Terry,
Keep Wat
for the 4.

DEAD MAN'S BLUES

Also by Jason Holscher

Lace & Whiskey
Temperance River

DEAD MAN'S BLUES

Jason Holscher

Dead Man's Blues

Copyright © 2012 by Jason Holscher

All rights reserved. No part of this book may be reproduced in any form or by any electronic or mechanical means, including information storage and retrieval systems, without permission in writing from the publisher, except by a reviewer who may quote brief passages in a review.

First Edition: April 2012

Manufactured in the United States of America

ISBN-13: 978-1468166620
ISBN-10: 146816662x

DEAD MAN'S BLUES

For my father...

And if we are to die tonight
Is there a moonlight up ahead?
And if we are to die tonight
Another rose will bloom.

— Tom Waits

Texas is a state of mind.

— John Steinbeck

Chapter 1

It was thundering outside when the phone rang. Robert Haywood was sleeping on his back in bed. The phone rang again and he opened his eyes and lifted his head off the pillow.

His wife was lying next to him on the big bed.

"What is it?" Annie whispered.

"Go back to sleep," Robert told her.

He reached for the phone without looking at it. The voice on the other line was scratchy and dry; half-familiar and half-forgotten:

"*Robert?*"

Robert's left hand was beating a tattoo on the side of the bed.

He said slowly: "Who is this?"

"*Robert, is that you...?*"

"Who the hell is this?"

There was a moment's pause at the other end of the line.

Then the voice said: "*This is your father.*"

Robert's eyes narrowed. The fingers of his left hand stopped beating and he became still.

He said: "Dad? Is this really you?"

"Yeah, it's me, son."

"What is it, Dad?" Robert asked, sitting up on the edge of the bed. Lightning cracked and the sky lighted up through the big bedroom window. "Are you all right?"

"I'm in some trouble, son."

"Where are you?"

"In jail."

"Is this some kind of bad joke, Dad?"

"No joke, son. I'm in jail."

"Where?"

"Some shit-hole border town called El Indio."

"Why were you arrested, Dad?"

When he said it, Annie shifted beside him on the big bed. She was giving him her famous *what in the hell is going on now?* look.

Robert glanced back at her and rolled his eyes.

Into the silence that followed, his father's voice echoed through the line. "I was in a fight. A bar fight. So they got me for drunken disorder, too. Or something like that. I owe some damages to the bar and all. Plus I got my car down here but I ain't got no license to drive it home. It was revoked last summer."

"Why are you telling me all this, Dad?" Robert heard himself asking in a strengthless little voice.

"I need you to come get me, son," his father said. "I need you to bail me out and drive me home."

"Drive you home? Do you mean you're coming back *here,* to Amarillo?"

"Yeah. I guess that's where I still call home."

Robert paused and swallowed hard. "I can't come get you, Dad," he finally said. "I got a job. I got a wife and kids to take care of. I can't just drop everything and come down to the border to bail you out of jail. Christ, I haven't even heard from you in almost two years, now you lay this on me?"

"Well, what do you want me to do, son, rot down here? I got no one else."

"No, I don't want you to rot down there, Dad," Robert said. He looked across the bed at Annie. She had that sour look on her face, the same look she always got when it involved his father. "I got responsibilities up here, you know," Robert said into the phone. "I got a job and a wife and kids. I got my own family now, Dad. What am I supposed to do about that?"

"I don't know, son," his father said. "But I'm up to my neck in a kettle of boiling shit down here and I don't know what else I can do."

"How much money are we talking about? For bail and all?"

"Two grand."

"Two grand! Where the hell am I supposed to come up with that kind of money?"

"I'll pay it all back, son. I promise I will. I'll get a job when I get back up there and I'll pay back every red cent, right down to the airfare and all your other expenses."

Robert went silent for a moment. He could feel Annie's eyes still boring down on him.

"All right, Dad," he sighed heavily and resignedly into the phone. "I'll see what I can do."

"Thanks, son."

There was a long pause. Then: "I love you."

A knot tightened in Robert's throat. His father hadn't said those three words to him since he was a kid.

I love you.

Hell, he couldn't remember his dad ever saying it.

Chapter 2

Robert waited for the click, then hung up. Annie was already sitting up on her side of the bed.

"You ain't going," she said.

Annie Haywood was a small Texas blonde with soft green eyes, a dabbling of freckles and the sweetest disposition of any woman Robert had ever known. But she could also get plenty tough when she felt she needed to, and right now she felt like she needed to.

"I have to go, honey," Robert said, reaching over to rub her shoulders. "He's got no one else."

"What kinda trouble has he gotten himself into now?"

"He's in jail. Got in some bar fight or something, and driving with a suspended license. I don't know what all else."

Annie sighed and blew frustration out the side of her thin lips. "When is that man going to grow up? Jesus Christ!"

Robert said: "He just hasn't been the same since my mom died."

Annie's green eyes snapped. "Hasn't been the same? Your father has been in trouble all his life, even when your mother *was* alive. The things that man put her through. It's a miracle she lived as long as she did. And all the excuses he had for his behavior. I never met a man with more excuses."

"What am I supposed to do, Annie?" Robert said, his voice rising. "You want me to let him rot down there? He's still my father, you know? He's still my own flesh and blood."

"Let him rot down there for all I care," she said. "Maybe it'd do him some good."

Robert got out of bed. He walked over to the dresser and took out a pack of cigarettes from the top drawer.

"I thought you weren't going smoke those things in the house no more," Annie said. "It ain't good for the kids."

"It ain't gonna kill 'em if I smoke one cigarette in the house," Robert said, lighting a Marlboro. He knew it wasn't a nice thing to say, but right now he needed a cigarette in a bad way.

"You're really an asshole sometimes," Annie said.

Robert blew the smoke out of his nostrils. "I don't want to fight, Annie. I just don't know what else to do."

"Can't you just wire him some money?"

"He's got his car down there and he needs me to drive it back."

"Why?"

"His license was revoked," Robert said, inhaling deeply on the cigarette.

"What about your job at the bank? What are you going to tell them?"

"I'll tell them something's come up. A family emergency or something. They'll understand. Hell, I haven't even taken a sick day in almost two years."

Robert stubbed out the cigarette in an empty Diet Coke can and walked over to his wife and sat beside her on the bed.

"I'm sorry; honey, but I don't know what else I can do. I don't want to go, but I have to."

"How the hell are we going to afford it, Robert? Did you think of that? We're struggling as it is just to live paycheck to paycheck. We've got car payments, insurance, utilities and the mortgage is almost three months late."

He looked hard at her. "How the hell did that happen?"

She shot him a look full of murder. "Don't ask me how that happened like it was my fault, Robert. It just happened. The point is we can't afford to be spending thousands of dollars on this right now."

Robert ran his fingers through Annie's long blonde hair. "He promised he'll pay it all back. For now, I'll take an advance out on the credit card."

"But the finance charges are already eating us alive," Annie said. "Pretty soon we'll have to file bankruptcy, Robert. Is that what you want?"

"We'll pay it all off before we get charged," he said, trying to calm her. He stroked her blonde hair some more and put a strand of it behind her ear.

"How are we going to pay it all off, Robert?" Annie said. "Are you going to get a second job?"

"Hey, c'mon, it'll be all right in the end, you'll see." He poked her gently in the ribs—her ticklish spot—and thought he saw a little flicker of a smile on her face.

An excruciating pause ensued. Seconds only, of course, but it seemed to Robert that the pyramids could have been built during that pause. Built and torn down again.

After a while, Annie said, "You're gonna go whether I want you to or not, ain't ya?"

"It'll only be for a few days. I promise. And when I get back I'll get a second job if that's what it takes. Then I'll take you downtown to Outlaws and we'll get a couple of those butter-knife steaks you love so much."

Annie looked up at him and gave him her pouty look. She knew it was useless to fight any longer. "You promise?"

"Yep. Cross my heart and hope to die."

"All right, you can go," she said, her face washed clean of expression, but her eyes were haunted. "I want you to stay out of trouble, Robert. I know how your dad gets."

He leaned over the bed and kissed her on the cheek. "Thanks, baby. I better go downstairs and see if I can arrange a flight."

He got up and started walking out of the room. When he was out in the hall he could hear Annie call out to him from the bed:

"You owe me...*big time,* buddy."

He smiled and went downstairs and walked through the cool dark house to the kitchen.

He grabbed a beer out of the refrigerator and went down to the basement where his computer was. After a few minutes of surfing the internet he found a cheap AirTran Airways commuter flight to Brownsville, Texas, the closest airport within a hundred miles of El Indio. When he was done charging the ticket to his credit card, he turned the computer off and went back upstairs and outside onto the front porch to finish his beer and have another cigarette. He knew he should quit these things; Annie didn't like it when he smoked, but it was hard. Damn hard. When his mother died a little more than five years ago, after a lifetime of putting down Camels like candy cigarettes, he had promised himself and Annie that he would quit, but every time a new problem would raise its ugly head, the urge to smoke would overtake him like a newborn baby being weaned from its mother's nipple.

He sat on the front stoop, in the yellow glow of the porch light, and inhaled deeply. The night was sweet with the smell of summer grasses and fresh like things right after a thunderstorm. The rain had finally died off and crickets were now chirping loudly in the long grass and the full moon was over the tops of the trees, glaring on the whitewash of houses and narrow streets, making the well-manicured lawns blaze softly.

Robert looked along the neat suburban street and the tidy roast-beef colored red-brick homes, and everything was perfect.

He knew he had a big mortgage to pay off on the house and that worried him a bit, but it was worth it to live here in this neighborhood. It was perfect. Perfect for the kids. Perfect for everything. Perfect and safe and happy.

He stood up and stretched and threw his cigarette in the bushes and went back inside the house.

Chapter 3

When Robert went back upstairs Annie was sleeping again. He went into the closet and packed his things into a black leather duffle bag as quietly as he could. Then he heard a faint noise behind him and when he turned around he saw his little girl Jenny standing in the doorway rubbing at her big sleepy eyes with her tiny fists.

"Whatcha doing, Daddy?" Jenny asked, yawning cavernously.

"I've got to go away for a few days, honey," Robert said. "How come you're up, pumpkin? Did I wake you?"

"Nuh-uh, Daddy. I just wasn't tired no more."

"You want to lay down in my bed next to Mamma for a while, sweetie?"

Jenny nodded her little head and smiled up at him. She was just about the cutest thing he had ever lay eyes on. She had her mother's good looks and the same bubbly blonde hair.

Robert picked her up in his arms and laid her softly on the bed next to Annie. He pulled the covers up to Jenny's chin and kissed her forehead and she smiled up at him again and he felt a curious rush of pride and love go through him as powerful as a wave at high tide.

"There now," he whispered. "Get some rest."

Jenny answered him with her big green eyes. They were so big and green and so full of devotion and life that Robert could have cried right there.

Jenny turned on her side, and nuzzled the blankets around her chin. Robert stood there looking down at his daughter and at that moment he didn't think it was possible to love something as much as he loved his kids. A love that almost pained him.

He went into the opposite bathroom and took a quick shower and then a shave and got dressed. When he went back out into the bedroom he saw his son Jack now in the bed, nestled happily between Annie and his sister Jenny.

The boy yawned sleepily. He was a toe-headed kid, with his grandfather's wild eyes and a thin skin which hinted of too much candy and too many ice cream shakes.

"Are you going to work today, Daddy?" Jack asked.

"No, son," Robert said. "I've got to go on a trip today."

"Where?" Jack said excitedly. "Where are you going, Daddy?"

"A place called El Indio. It's by Mexico. Ever hear of Mexico before?"

Jack nodded his head. "I read about it in school. It's big. And wild and they kill people there."

The boy had started third grade last fall and it worried Robert a little what they were teaching them these days. Or maybe it was the TV. He tried to limit what his kids took in, but every time you turned on the local news they were talking about all the murders on the border and the drug cartels pushing their violence slowly northward.

"How long you gonna be gone, Daddy?" Jack asked, with a note of longing on his little voice.

"Only for a few days," Robert said. He paused for a moment, and then went on. "I'm going to pick up your grandpa, and bring him home. Do you remember your Grandpa Haywood?"

"No. But I remember seeing pictures of him. Is he going to live with us, Dad?"

Robert thought it over for a moment. "I don't know, son."

Jack held out his arms and gave his father a big hug. "I don't want you to go, Daddy," he said. "I want you to stay here with Mom and me and Jenny and baby Grace."

"I wish I could, son," Robert said. "But it's okay. I won't be gone long. You've got to take care of your sisters and your mom for me while I'm away. You'll be the man of the house when I'm gone. Think you're up for the job?"

Jack smiled proudly.

"Good," Robert said, pulling the blankets over him. "Now, get some rest. It's still early and you've got to go to school today."

"Okay, Dad," Jack said, resting his head on the pillow. "I love you."

"I love you too, son."

Robert smiled and picked up his black duffle bag. He went out of the room quietly and down the hall to the nursery where his youngest daughter was still sleeping in her crib. He stood over the crib for a moment and watched her in her twitching infant sleep, her hand bunching around his finger.

He leaned down and kissed her perfect lips, her mouth just the tiniest pucker.

"I love you, baby Grace," he whispered. "I'll see you soon."

He tiptoed out of the room and went downstairs into the quiet kitchen. He put two scoops into the coffee pot and plopped a few slices of wheat bread in the toaster. Then he picked up the phone and called the bank where he worked. He knew his boss wouldn't like it when he told him he needed to be out of the office for a few days. He hadn't called in sick or taken a vacation day in almost two years, but still, Mr. Longwell, the bank President, wasn't going to like it. Especially during their busy season.

When Longwell answered the phone Robert spoke quickly and calmly, trying to conceal his nervousness.

"What do you mean you won't be coming in to work today?" Longwell said. His plaintive, fretful voice held a thread of hot despair and a touch of disappointment.

Longwell was short, plump and crowding sixty. He had pure white hair topping a pink cherubic face, and with the deep permanent creases of wealthy laughter lines radiating from his eyes and curving round his mouth, he always reminded Robert of Mr. Moneybags from the board game *Monopoly*. Mr. Moneybags with a felt Stetson.

"I need a few days off, sir," Robert repeated. He knew Longwell was annoyed, and he said, without thinking: "Sorry, sir, but it's not my fault, you know. A family emergency has come up."

"Is Annie okay?" Longwell asked, his hot voice changing quickly and genuinely to concern. "I hope nothing's wrong with the kids or something?"

"No, sir, they're all fine," Robert said. "But thanks for your concern."

"Well, what is it then?"

"It's my father, sir," Robert said in a thick voice. "I've got to straighten a few things out. I'll be back to work first thing Monday morning."

There was a quality to the silence, a heaviness that felt almost fatal.

"Well, all right then," Longwell finally said. "I guess a man's got to do what a man's got to do."

"Thank you, sir," Robert said. "See you Monday."

"Bright and early I hope," Longwell said and hung up the phone.

Robert sat there for a while, then poured himself a big mug of coffee and put butter and jelly on his toast and sat down to read the morning paper.

"Anything interesting in there?"

Annie had snuck up close behind him. Her arms crept forward around his shoulders, and clung there. She pressed her cheek against his back, tightly, and held it there.

"What are you doing up?" Robert asked. "I thought you were still sleeping?"

"I was. But I couldn't let you go without saying goodbye. You still are going, aren't you?"

Robert nodded his head. "Yes."

"I wish you wouldn't."

"I know."

Annie came around him and took a bite of his toast and Robert wiped the jelly off the side of her lips.

"Are the kids still sleeping?" he asked.

She nodded, smiling, almost eagerly. "Yes. They're still sleeping."

"Do you want to—?"

"What? Right here?" Annie asked, blushing. She had an ear cocked for the kids, but so far they were still sleeping like lambs.

"Why not?" Robert said with a certain strained tense passion.

"What if they wake up?"

"We'll hear 'em coming down the stairs."

Robert kissed her and she kissed him back, laughing with a kind of sweet resignation that caused his whole heart to fall in love with her all over again.

She put her arms around him and whispered in his ear. "You're crazy."

"I know," he said, and hugged her tight and kissed the hollow of her throat.

Their lips merged again and he felt her good body in the thin white nightgown and her breasts against his chest and her soft lips tight against his. Her head was moving from side to side, and her breathing was coming low and hard. He felt his belt buckle against his belly and in her hands.

He lifted the nightgown over her head and dropped it to the floor. She had him in her hands now and he felt her bare breasts against his chest as they made love on the kitchen floor and when they were finished Annie whispered, "Will you kiss me again, Robert Haywood, so that I won't be lonely while you're gone?"

Chapter 4

He tried calling Annie once on his cell phone from the plane but she didn't answer.

The answering machine on the kitchen counter picked up after the fourth ring and Annie's jovial voice buzzed out of the receiver: "Hi, you've reached the Haywood's. We're unable to answer the phone right now, but if you leave your name and number we'll call you back as soon as we can. Thanks."

"Hey, it's me..." Robert said into the machine. "I just wanted to see how you're doing. I'll call you back when I land in Brownsville. Bye."

He turned off his cell. The stewardess came around again and brought him a green tea. She was cute and rather young and he thought for a moment that she was flirting with him, but he knew it was just a case of wishful thinking springing up from his thirty-five year old married man's heart. Not that he would have done anything about it if she *had* been flirting with him. He loved Annie very much and in the eight years they had been married he never even once thought about cheating on her. It just wasn't worth it in the long run. He couldn't even dream of hurting Annie like that, or the kids. That was the problem with the world today, everyone was in it for themselves, and nobody gave a damn about how their actions might affect others around them, even the one's closest to them.

Robert grabbed an in-flight magazine from the pouch on the back of the seat in front of him, and when the guy plopped down into the seat beside him, he just glanced up and then turned back to the magazine again. The plane left the ground and began climbing, and Robert looked back through the small oval window and saw the tarmac drop away below him.

"An airplane ride is just like marriage," the guy sitting next to him said.

Robert looked up from the magazine. The man was fat and sweaty with little pink eyes that were embedded deep in soft, ruddy flesh. He was wearing Bermuda shorts and black socks and a sweat-stained T-shirt declaring: DONT MESS WITH TEXAS and his breath reeked of airport Big Mac.

The fat man chuckled. "I say an airplane ride is just like a marriage. Lots of ups and downs, and not always too smooth—but guaranteed to keep a man up in the air."

Robert smiled politely, and the fat man cleared his throat and chuckled a bit more.

"A wonderful institution; marriage, but who likes being in an institution?"

He laughed aloud and Robert began to wonder if he was going to be treated to the fat man's full stockpile of threadbare jokes before the trip was over. To discourage any further attempts at misdirected banter, he turned back to the magazine as politely as he could, smiling once to let the fat man know he wasn't being purposely rude.

He finished his magazine and his tea and the motion of the plane made him sleepy. His eyes soon grew heavy; too heavy to keep open any longer. He closed them mercifully and fell into a deep sleep.

He must have slept for a few hours because when he woke up again the sun's shadow was on the other side of the plane. Then it tipped once on its wings and began its slow descent through the big puffy white clouds.

Robert glanced out the window and saw the brown scorched desert and the contrasting blue waters of Lake Casa Blanca. In another fifteen minutes they'd be touching down in Brownsville.

He was one of the last ones off the plane and when he stepped into the windowless terminal of Brownsville International, he could immediately feel the change in temperature. The state of Texas is a big place, and from Amarillo to Brownsville it was almost 800 miles, and the air itself had changed. It was damn hot down here.

Robert pushed and prodded his way toward the baggage claim and waited for what seemed like an eternity for the octopus-like machine to spit out his black leather duffle. Then he went out the door to the "arrivals" zone and got on a packed trolley bus and it was hot and uncomfortable in there, too. He was crammed between a fat, sweaty middle-aged tourist from Iowa and a rich, rather annoyed-looking Texan in a ten-gallon hat.

The trolley dropped them off at a Dollar Rental Car where Robert went in and rented a Chevy Malibu and charged it to his ever-ballooning Visa card. He felt tired and grimy as he drove out of the parking lot.

Turning south he followed the exit signs to Highway 83. It was oppressively hot inside the rental car so he cranked the air conditioning all the way and he turned on the radio, but all he could find was some twangy Texas bullshit. He moved the tuner up and down the dial but all he was getting was Country. He finally settled on a station that was playing an old Wanda Jackson tune and he kept the car steady on 83 toward the little town of El Indio.

It was just a speck on the Rand McNally. He wondered how his father ever wound up in a town like *El Indio.*

Robert was a little nervous about seeing his father again after all these years, and he really didn't know how he was going to handle the reunion.

He loved his dad, but Annie was dead-on when she said he'd been a burden to the family all his life.

Robert had been driving for almost two hours and the sun was just starting to set when he finally saw the green exit signs for El Indio. He pulled off the Interstate and followed the narrow dusty frontage road until it came to the town line.

He crept the car slowly into town, passing a billboard on the side of the road that read: *El Indio—The Loveliest Village on the Plains.*

The dusty narrow streets were full of Mexican boys in cowboy hats and cowboy boots practicing their roping skills on dummy steers set up in the front yards.

The frontage eventually snaked into Main Street, where men in wide-brimmed cowboy hats staggered along the sidewalks looking for a cool place to grab a beer while Mexican women and their small children rushed about madly.

Small businesses lined both sides of the street: a barber shop, a bakery, a Laundromat/movie store, a gas station, a Mexican restaurant called *Buena Comida,* and a thrift shop.

Robert pulled the car over to the side of the road and asked a weather-beaten Mexican if he knew his way around town.

"*Sí señor,*" the old man said.

"Could you tell me where I could find the local police station?" Robert asked.

The old man looked at him questioningly, then pointed to the end of the street and told him in Spanish to go left.

Robert thanked him and pulled back out onto Main Street, took a left at the corner and saw a small square building on the right hand side.

A weathered sign hung above the door advertising the El Indio Police Department. The old building looked like it had been built by veterans of the Spanish-American War. It was two stories of old white brick with about a hundred and seventy years of dirt on it.

Robert parked the rented Malibu next to a few beat-up squad cars and went in.

Sitting behind a desk was a rather large Mexican woman wearing a police uniform two sizes too small for her. She had her head bent and was reading a *Vanidades* magazine, her chubby right hand sneaking out periodically to grab the *Submarino* cakes off her cluttered desk.

Robert cleared his throat.

She ignored him.

"Excuse me," he said, "I'm here to pick up my father."

She finally looked up. Her brown, sweaty face was annoyed as she folded the magazine and set it down on the messy desk.

She said in a heavy Spanish accent: "What's your father's name?"

"Dick Haywood," Robert said. "Richard Haywood."

"Ah-h, he in back. You come to pay fine and take him out?"

"Yes, that's right."

"It will cost you plenty," the woman said, and Robert thought he saw a little smirk run away from her fat, wet lips.

"Exactly how much will it cost?" he asked.

She reached across the filing cabinet and took up a manila folder and bent over it. She took out a sheet of paper and smirked again as she started reading:

"Your father's been arrested for drunk and disorderly conduct, driving with a suspended license, public intoxication and resisting arrest. The owner of the cantina he wrecked was nice enough not to press charges, as long as he pays for expenses. Of course, your father won't be able to drive with a suspended license."

"I'll pay all the expenses," Robert said. "How much is it?"

The woman looked down at the sheet of paper and her big bosoms shook as she coughed up a piece of her Submarino cake. "With the fines and damages to the cantina, the grand total comes to two thousand eighty-four dollars and sixty three cents. Exactly."

"Jesus," Robert said. "That's highway robbery,"

"*Sí señor,*" the fat woman said with another smirk. Then she went on: "Your father's a *desmadroso*. He's lucky to have someone like you to get him out of his jams..."

Robert took out his checkbook and began writing a check.

"Con permiso, señor," the woman said. "No checks, por favor. Cash or credit."

"Jesus," Robert said again, handing her his Visa.

"Gracias."

She slid his card through a manual carbon copy imprinter and handed him the folded yellow receipt.

"Un momento," she said, the slash of fat lips forming something like a smile.

She took his father's paperwork and disappeared through a door behind her desk. A few minutes later she returned with a short Texan in a dark police uniform wearing a half-gallon hat and lizard-skin cowboy boots.

The Texan's face was tight, his eyes mean, and he had a plug of tobacco stuck in the side of his cheek with a mouth that was much tighter than a simple tobacco chewer's mouth needed to be.

Handcuffed to the short Texan was a skinny man with thick, ruffled white hair and a two-day growth of white whiskers.

The handcuffed man's face was a calm face, tanned deeply, but with scars and heavy lines that seemed to convey a rough, copious life. The edges of his teeth were tipped in gold. His shackled hands were extremely long-fingered, adorned by numerous silver rings, axle grease, and a black and blue thumb.

It took Robert a moment to realize that this man was his father.

"*Junior!*" his father said with a slanted smile, and his gold teeth glittered. "I knew I could count on you, son."

"Hello, Dad," Robert said.

Dick Haywood turned to the short Texan and held up his shackled hands. "Take the nippers off, you big monkey."

The short Texan glared at him for a moment, then took out a set of keys and unlocked the handcuffs.

Dick Haywood rubbed his wrists for a second, then he walked over and hugged Robert tightly.

"How you been, son?" he whispered into Robert's ear.

"I was doing just fine, until you called," Robert said, but deep down it felt good to see his old man again. He couldn't deny that.

Before Robert could take his father out of jail the large Mexican woman made him fill out a stack of papers the size of Mount Hood.

As they were leaving, Dick Haywood smiled at the fat Mexican woman, and said to the short Texan: "Take 'er easy, and if she's easy *amigo,* take 'er twice."

His laugh was wild and unsettling. Out in the parking lot the desert breeze was blowing and the stars were winking down at them through gray clouds.

"Where do we pick up your car?" Robert asked his father.

"They got her down at the impound lot on Mission Street. It's just around the corner there."

"Well, let's get going then. I want to get back on the road as soon as possible."

"What's your rush, son?"

"I got a family waiting for me back home," Robert said, a little surprised by the rough edge of fury in his voice. "In case you forgot."

"I didn't forget," his father said. "How's Annie doing anyway? I always did like that little girl. She a good little wife."

"Annie's doing fine, Dad. Now let's go."

Dick Haywood stopped and looked over his son, head to boot and back again. "Wedlock suits you," he remarked. "Looks like you put on about ten pounds since I saw you last."

Robert ignored the comment and they got in the rented Malibu and drove the few blocks to the impound lot on Mission Street. Robert went into the office and filled out another mountain of paperwork. He arranged for the rental car to be picked up at the lot, then he grabbed his father and they went out and searched for his father's car.

"There she is," Dick Haywood said, pointing to a red 1966 Chevy Impala convertible.

Robert stared at the car and his jaw dropped so far it almost fell on the fender. It was the kind of car every guy in high school would have killed for. Shiny and red with chrome fenders and leather upholstery.

"Nice car, Dad," Robert said. "Where'd you manage to steal a car like that?"

His father gave him another gold-capped smile. "Didn't steal it, son. Won it in a poker game."

Robert opened the driver's side door and sank into the red leather upholstery. His father got in next to him. Robert put the key in the ignition and fired it up. It sounded like a lion purring. He lifted the parking brake and drove out of the impound lot.

He drove slowly out of town and once he got up on the interstate he kept the car stroking at an even 65 m.p.h. His father flashed a smile and reached inside the glove compartment and started rummaging around in there.

"Ahhh, the *motherfucker's* didn't find it," he said, taking out a pint of Wild Turkey that was hiding underneath some old yellowed highway maps.

He took a long noisy gulp of the mud-colored liquid and closed his eyes as though he was in ecstasy, or dreaming of a woman he once loved a long time ago.

"Ah, that's good," he said, holding out the bottle to Robert. "You want a little nip, son?"

"No."

"Why not? You a teetotaler?"

"No. I just don't drink and drive."

"Hell, this is Texas, son. Everybody in Texas drinks and drives. Besides, there's hardly ever a soul on this stretch of highway. One little nip won't kill ya."

Robert glanced over at him. "This ain't a goddamn frat party, Dad."

"Lighten up, son. You've gotten too damn highfalutin. But I guess that's what the married life will do to a man after a few years."

"Is that right, Dad? Is that how you see it? Is that why you kept running away when I was a kid and leaving Mom to do all the work?"

"*You just watch your mouth!*" The edge in Dick Haywood's voice was like a whiplash loaded with tiny pellets of buckshot. "I'm still your father you know."

"So when are you going to start acting like it?"

His father took a pack of Lucky Strikes from his shirt pocket and lit one. He took a long delicious pull and allowed the smoke to very slowly creep out through his hairy nostrils and the dark corner of his mouth.

"Yeah, I guess you're right, son. I guess I should have worn out my knees in church more than I did. I never was much of a father. I loved your mother and I always loved you, but I got rambling feet, son. When they say go, I got to go with 'em. I've always had a lust for wandering. Something akin to the migratory instinct in birds and quadrupeds."

Robert gave him a look like he was crazy and drove in silence, listening to the radio which was still blaring out some crappy Country Western songs. He was staring out the dusty windshield at the blackened highway, awash with a thin strip of light from the Impala's head beams. There were no other cars on the road. The landscape around them was dark, empty.

Then, finally and if out of the blue, his father said, "There's a little town up ahead called Carrizo Springs. Maybe we could stop in and have ourselves a bite to eat. I know a little place where they serve the best steaks this side of the Rio Grande. Whatta say, son?"

"Like I said before, Dad, I want to get back to Amarillo as soon as possible. It's about a two-day drive and I ain't fucking around."

His father shrugged. "We gotta eat, son. Besides, you planning on driving all night?"

"Maybe."

"You're liable to fall asleep and get us both killed," his father said, flicking the ashes of his cigarette out the open window. "I'm hungry! If I had known you were gonna starve me to death I would've had second thoughts about asking you to bail me out. I coulda always got supper back in the can. Three hots and a cot, as they say. Come on, son. We gotta eat sometime."

Robert knew the old man could talk a cat into barking, but he was starting to feel hunger rumbling in his own belly.

"All right," he said.

"*Tenemos fiesta!*" his father shouted. "We'll eat good. *Comeremos bien.*"

Robert looked over at him. "When did you learn to speak Spanish?"

His father winked at him. "I'm a man of many talents, son. A man of many talents."

"What did you say the name of this town was?"

"Carrizo Springs. It's just off the interstate."

Robert took the next exit to Carrizo Springs and followed the road signs toward Main Street.

"There it is," his father said.

He was pointing one of his long dirty fingers across the road to a small bar with Lone Star beer neons shining from the windows.

The place was called the Longhorn Tavern and when they walked in, Robert's ears were ravished by loud Merle Haggard music blaring out of the jukebox and raucous laughter coming from the drunk cowboys sitting bowlegged around the long bar.

The bartender knew Robert's father and he set them up with a couple tallboys of Lone Star. The beer tasted good and Robert finished his before his father.

"Geez, son, take it easy," his father said with a dry scratchy laugh. "I thought you was planning on driving all night?"

The bartender set two more glistening tallboys in front of them and they ordered a couple Porterhouse specials with tortillas and *frijoles refritos.*

While they waited for their food they sat at the long bar and drank their beers. Robert's father pulled over a big bowl of peanuts and placed it between them. He was trying to get friendly. Robert could hear it in his voice. Trying to include him in something, as though he was one of his old drinking buddies. But the more he tried, the further Robert felt from him. At that moment, he had memories of the long nights in their small kitchen on Cherry Avenue, his father sucking down countless bottles of *Shiner* beer and listening to ZZ Top LPs on his beloved Pioneer turntable, his mother laughing along and dancing until the kitchen counter was amok with empty beer bottles and numerous cigarette butts and the laughter and dancing inevitably dissolving into screams and threats of violence so obscene that Robert would retreat to his upstairs bedroom and cover his head beneath the blankets until he eventually and mercifully fell asleep.

"So how are those grandkids of mine?" his father said, his deep voice dragging Robert back into the present with all the force of a two-fisted grip. "They must be growing like weeds."

"You haven't even met baby Grace yet," Robert said, the beer loosening his tongue a bit. "She's only eight months old. Jenny's six and Jack's eight. He started third grade in the fall."

"You got pictures?"

Robert pulled out his wallet from the back of his jeans and handed it to his father.

"They're mighty fine looking kids," his father said, flipping slowly through the pictures. "The boy, Jack, he looks like *us*."

"Like us?" Robert asked.

"You and me. He's just like *us*, with something mean in his look. He had to get some of that from me."

"He ain't mean," Robert said, taking back his wallet and sticking it in his jeans. "He's the sweetest little boy around."

His father sipped his beer. "You ain't teaching him to be a mama's boy, are ya?"

Robert shrugged. "He's tough enough when he has to be."

"That's good," his father said, his voice soft, but almost deadly emphatic. "Because nowadays everybody is raising their boys to be fairies. That's why everything's so fucked up in the world. Boys don't know how to be boys no more."

Their steaks came and the bartender slid a few more tallboys in front of them. Robert had to be careful because the beer was going down damn good now and he didn't want to get a buzz going. He wanted to get back on the road and maybe get in another hundred or so miles yet tonight.

"How's your steak?" his father asked, between bites.

"It's good," Robert said, and he wasn't lying. Pure Aberdeen Angus.

"I told you. If you had it your way you would have stopped at one of those convenience stores for some potato chips and a couple microwavable sandwiches or something."

They devoured the steaks, and when they were finished, Robert paid the bill and they walked out and across the narrow street to the Impala shining like a lost gemstone under a streetlamp. Robert fell in behind the wheel and started it up. His father got in and lit a cigarette.

"You got one of those for me?" Robert asked.

"You smoke, son?"

"Now and then."

"I would have never taken you for a smoker," his father said, lighting one for Robert and handing it over.

Robert took a drag and turned the big car back toward the interstate.

The highway was deserted and he was a little more relaxed because he was still feeling the effects of the three tallboys they just drank back at the bar. The night breeze blew through the car and it felt fine.

"You ever been to Mexico, son?" his father asked.

"Yeah, once," Robert said, not sure where his father was going with this one. "Me and Annie spent our honeymoon in Cancun."

"Cancun ain't Mexico!" his father said, smiling, sort of absent and loose. "Not the *real* Mexico. Cancun is a Spanish Disneyland dreamed up by a bunch of rich American cocksuckers. I'm talking about the real Mexico." He paused here for a moment, and then his voice took on a clandestine tone: "You know we're only a few miles from the border. I know a road that dips down into *Ol' Mehico!* The wetbacks use it to sneak into the country. No one else knows about it."

Robert looked down meditatively for a moment, then up at his father again.

"Yeah, so?"

"Well, I thought maybe we could pop on down there and get ourselves another drink. There's a little town there I like to go to sometimes."

"Forget about it, Dad," Robert said. "You can just get that little brainstorm out of your head right quick. Besides, even if I was half-interested, you can't leave the country now. You're out on bail, remember? What if a cop pulled us over?"

"There ain't any cops on *this* road."

"Forget it, Dad."

"Okay, okay," his father said, holding up his hands. "It's just, I got myself a little *señorita* down there and since I'm leaving and won't ever be back, I thought it might be nice to give her my farewells. That's all."

Robert looked over at him. "You have a girlfriend in Mexico?"

"Sure do. Best damn woman I ever had. 'Cepting for your mother, of course."

Robert gripped the steering wheel hard and he could feel his father's reptilian eyes upon him.

"No way, Dad," he finally said. "I want to make good time and I can't afford to be fucking around down in Mexico."

There was a kind of beat in the conversation then—not quite a pause. Then Robert looked at his watch and swore under his breath.

"What's the matter?" his father asked.

"I forgot to call Annie. I told her I would call when I got to Brownsville."

"So call her now," his father said, looking off into the black desert. "Ain't you got one of those fancy little cell phones everybody carries around these days?"

"It's too late. The kids are probably in bed."

His father shrugged and Robert continued driving west on Highway 83, the interstate dead this time of night. The wind was blowing hard, but it was still god-awful hot. The car was so hot Robert's ears began to ring, and beads of sweat dotted the down above his lip.

"You know," his father said, "we're only a few miles from that border. Sure you won't let me say goodbye to my little *señorita?* She'll be awful sad to see me go without giving her my farewells."

Robert let out a sigh and rubbed his hand through his hair. He knew it was crazy, and maybe it was the effects of the three tallboys, but he was actually starting to think about it.

Don't you ever learn, he wrangled with himself. *Don't you know any better than to do what you're thinking of doing?*

Then he went ahead and did it anyway.

"What's the name of this town, Dad?"

"Durango," his father said.

"I thought Durango was on the other side of the coast?"

"This ain't *that* Durango. This is the *first* Durango. The *real* Durango. It's only about ten miles past the border. A small town of about three hundred wetbacks."

"What's your girlfriend's name?" Robert asked.

"Angelina."

It was a pretty name. Robert had to admit that.

"So, you gonna let me go see her?" his father asked.

A bare moment later Robert heard himself saying, "I suppose. But we ain't staying more than ten minutes. I want to get back on this interstate and start heading *north* for chrissakes."

Chapter 5

Annie Haywood wasn't all that worried when Robert hadn't called. In fact, she hadn't even thought about it that much. Hell, what with running the kids around, making dinner, giving them baths and putting them to bed, she didn't have time to think about anything at all.

But now, as she sat alone in their big empty bed, it was all she could do not to think about it.

Why hadn't Robert called her back?

He said on his message that he was going to call her when he landed in Brownsville. But he never did. And now it was well past midnight. Where the hell was he and what was he doing?

She was trying to read a book her mother loaned her, some trashy novel that Oprah Winfrey had endorsed on her television show, but Annie just couldn't concentrate.

Why hadn't he called her?

Maybe he got in an accident? Maybe he was lying in a ditch somewhere, slowly bleeding to death?

She turned the page of her book.

Where was he? Why didn't he call?

Maybe he just forgot.

Yeah, that was probably it. What with picking up his crazy old father and bailing him out of jail, he probably just forgot to call. He'll call first thing in the morning.

She kept telling herself that, trying not to think of Robert hurt or in some kind of trouble. He was really just a naïve kid at heart. He trusted people too much. That was his problem.

She turned the page of her book again.

He'll call tomorrow.

Chapter 6

They pulled off the interstate and onto a little dirt road that didn't even have a name. It was a road not on any GPS and it sure the hell wasn't on any Rand McNally. Robert would have missed it if his father hadn't pointed it out to him in the dark night.

He turned the car quickly off the interstate and blew a cloud of dust up as they hit the narrow ingress. It was little more than a washboard trail, two tortured, twisting ruts that snaked through the desert across the wasteland of the Piedras Negras Valley.

"We in Mexico yet?" Robert asked his father, as he peered through the two cones of light that the high beams threw off.

"Yep."

"I didn't see any signs."

"The locals down here don't do a lot of advertising," his father said, a hard flash in his eyes. "They like to keep it to themselves."

This was fucking crazy.

Robert knew he shouldn't have trusted his father. He should have just stayed on the interstate and found a Motel 6. All he could do now was follow his father's directions, and he began to feel a slight panic at the thought of getting lost out here in the desert without a soul around for miles. They had already forked off at two or three different crossroads; crossroads with no signposts of any kind.

The road narrowed until it was only wide enough for one thing going one way. Robert strained his eyes out the dirty windshield for some kind of distinguishing features, but the buttes in the distance all looked the same in the heavy darkness and the dust was lifting off the desert and driving gray spirals into the air like sluggish smoke.

"Where they hell are we?" he asked his father, trying not to sound too panicky.

"It's just right up there a bit, son."

Robert drove on and the only light came from a sickle moon that hung high up in the sky. After a while he finally saw a small town up ahead, if you could call it that. A gas station, a general store that was shut up for the night, a Catholic church, a couple of old bars with ancient *Modello* signs hanging in the windows.

"There it is," his father said, pointing out the window at a roadside shack called The White Horse Tavern.

"How do you know she's even in there?" Robert asked.

"She's always there," his father said.

Robert pulled the car over and they got out and started walking across the gravel driveway.

The moon was high in the black sky, playing peek-a-boo with the gray clouds and the wind was blowing the dust all around their ankles. The silence of the night was immense—there was only the wind and the sound of their boots crunching on the dusty driveway.

"Ten minutes, Dad," Robert said. "That's all you get in there. Then I want to get back on that damn interstate."

His father swung open the heavy door of the cantina and they went in.

It was almost empty, but hot from the wood stove in the corner and full of stale smoke. An old Wurlitzer jukebox was squawking out Mexican polkas, turned low the way it is when no one is listening. The old men in sombreros sitting at the bar didn't even look up from their beers or whiskey. It was late and almost everyone had left except a few old-timers and a group of three young Mexicans in the corner wearing soccer jerseys and shooting pool.

A woman was tending the place. She was a plump *señora* with a lovely ruddy complexion and black, curly hair, wearing a black leather skirt and a hot pink blouse that bolstered her large breasts. Hunks of turquoise set in gold clanked around her neck like a fortune teller.

Robert's father walked quickly over to the whiskey-colored bar and when the woman saw him she let out an uninhibited laugh.

"Hola, amigo!" she nearly screamed. "*Que tal?*"

"I'm doing fine, Angelina. And thou?"

"Alive."

Robert's father leaned over the bar and kissed the woman on the cheek. It was the first time Robert had seen him kiss a woman other than his mother.

"Where you been, *mi vida?*" the woman asked his father.

"Oh, around," he said. "Mostly up in Texas."

"I missed you so much."

"I know."

"*Quién es?*" the woman asked, pointing a big finger over at Robert.

"That's my son I was telling you about."

She smiled and stared at him.

"He's a handsome one, this young *Devil*. Sit, sit! I pour you cerveza."

She took two tall glasses and held them under the tap. "Are you staying this time, amigo?"

Dick Haywood shook his head. "Afraid not, sweetheart."

"That's what I was worried about," Angelina said. "So this is our goodbye then?"

"Yep."

"Well," Angelina sighed, holding up her meaty arms, "I guess that's what happens when I take up with the *Devil.*"

"I'm going home, Angelina, where I belong," Dick Haywood said, and smiled sadly.

"You write?" she asked.

"I'll write you all the time."

"Sure, sure. That's what all the *gringos* say."

Dick Haywood laughed and the three young Mexicans playing pool called out to him in Spanish. He looked up and smiled, or frowned, Robert couldn't tell which. Meanwhile, the old men in sombreros at the other end of the bar got up and left.

"I'll be right back," he said to Robert, taking his beer and walking over to the pool table.

Robert watched him talking to the three Mexicans and at first the conversation seemed friendly enough, but after a while it looked like they were arguing about something.

"They call him *El Pichón,*" Angelina said in a low voice.

"Excuse me?" Robert asked.

"Your papi. The people around here call him El Pichón. But he's no bandito or a killer. He's a good man."

"Have you known my father long?" Robert asked. He was still keeping his eyes on the discussion his father was having with the three young Mexicans.

"Si," Angelina said. "I met him in here over a year ago. How do you *Americano's* say it? He swept me off my toes?"

"Swept you off your feet," Robert corrected her with a little smile.

"Yes! Yes! He swept me off my feet."

After a few minutes his father came back to the bar and sat down.

"What was that all about?" Robert asked.

"Oh, those boys think I owe 'em some money," his father said with a wave of his hand.

"Do you?" Robert asked.

"Do I what?"

"Do you owe them money?"

"Hell no! That's just the way it is down here, son. People always think you owe them something. It was just a little poker game I got into one time. No big deal."

"*El Pichón,*" Angelina said to Robert with a big smile. "I told you so."

"What have you been telling him?" Dick Haywood asked.

Angelina smiled her big brown smile. "That I love you, amigo."

"I love you too, *mi vida.*" He took a sip of his beer, and then leaned forward over the wet bar, and whispered, "You still got that *cosas* I gave you?"

Angelina nodded her head. "*Si.*"

"Well, where is it?"

"Aqui."

She reached down behind the bar and brought up a faded green army sling duffle. Then she handed it over the bar to Robert's father. He put it over his shoulder and smiled.

"You're a good girl, Angelina. I'm gonna miss you something awful."

"You write?"

"I write," he said, a certain yearning wistfulness in his eyes. "*No llores, mi querida.*"

"*Agarrame, mi vida.*"

Dick Haywood leaned over the bar again and gave Angelina a long kiss.

"*Dio nos vigila,*" he told her.

Then he turned back to Robert.

"You ready, son?" he asked, and Robert sensed a certain sadness in his father's dry scratchy voice.

"Goodbye, Angelina," Robert said,shaking her hand. "It was a real pleasure to meet you."

"Si, Roberto. You make sure to keep your papi out of trouble. You hear?"

"I will," Robert said with a smile.

"He'll try," his father said, with another one of his discerning laughs.

They left the bar and got into the Impala and Robert turned it around back toward the little dirt road.

His father sat quietly in the passenger seat. He took out a cigarette and blew the smoke out the window. Another silence fell among them. It was short...but very, very heavy.

"What's in the bag?" Robert asked after a while.

"Huh?"

"The duffle Angelina gave you. What's in it?"

His father looked down at the faded duffle bag at his feet. "Just some old stuff of mine. Mementos and what not."

Robert looked at him for a moment. Then he turned his eyes back on the dark, tortured and twisting road in front of them.

They had a long way to get back home...

Chapter 7

"What the hell is *that?*" Robert said, looking in the rear view mirror.

His father draped an arm over the back of the red velvet seat of the Impala.

"Headlights. Looks like someone's following us."

"Why the hell would someone be following us way out here?"

Robert looked in the rear view mirror again and could see the headlights of the other car getting closer, busting down the dusty road at a steady clip.

"Is it the cops?" he said in a low voice.

His father jerked his skinny head around again, his eyes gleaming in the dark interior of the car.

"Don't know," he said. "But there's not many *federales* that know about this road."

"Who is it then?" Robert said, feeling a bit panicky now. "They're getting damn close."

He knew he should have never listened to his father. He should have just stayed on that damn interstate.

"It ain't the cops," his father said, staring out the back window.

"Who is it then?"

His father paused. "It's Esteban," he finally said in a cool voice.

"Who the fuck's *Esteban?*"

"One of those boys back at the bar. Looks like he's brought his friends with him, too."

"*What?*"

Robert looked in the rear view mirror again. The headlights of the other car were right behind them now.

"What do they want?" he asked with a muffled sound in his voice, as though he held something soft between his teeth and talked through it.

"Don't know," his father said. "Why don't you pull over and find out?"

"No way. No fucking way. I ain't pulling over on this road in the damn dark."

"You yellow, son?"

"Shut up, Dad. This ain't some goddamn John Wayne movie!"

His father smiled and kept looking out the back window, blowing smoke through his nostrils. "They're flashing their lights at us, son."

"What do they want? I'm not pulling over. They can follow us all the way to the interstate if they want."

"I reckon they won't do that."

Robert looked in the rear view mirror again. "Jesus! They're getting close."

Then a thud ripped through the back of the car.

"They fucking rammed us!" Robert shouted. "They fucking hit us!"

"You better stop the car, son."

"Fuck that!"

They felt another thud. This time a little harder.

"Jesus!" Robert almost screamed.

"They ain't gonna quit until you stop the car, son."

"What do they want?"

His father smiled again and Robert noticed the blackening edges of his gold teeth. "Let's find out."

Robert thought about it for a moment. He didn't know how far it was to the interstate. Maybe a few more miles, probably more.

Maybe they could make it.

Another thud. This time it was so hard it jerked Robert's neck and rattled his teeth.

"Fuck!" he shouted, hammering at the steering wheel with his fists.

"Pull over, son," his father said.

"No fucking way!"

"They're just gonna keep ramming us."

Robert thought about it some more, then he reluctantly slammed on the brakes and watched in the rear view as the car behind them screeched to a halt, barely missing their rear fender, sending up a thick black cloud of dust.

Robert sat there for a moment and watched the car behind them, but no one got out. Nothing moved except the dust.

"I'll be right back," his father finally said, opening the passenger door.

"Where are you going?"

"I'll take care of this. You stay here, son."

"You can't go out there alone," Robert said, reaching for his father's arm.

"Why not?"

"I don't know," Robert said. "What's this all about, Dad?"

"I reckon it's about the money they think I owe them."

"I got money, Dad. Just pay them what they want and let's get the fuck out of here."

"I told you I don't owe those wetbacks nothing. You just stay in the car and let me talk to 'em."

Dick Haywood got out and walked behind the Impala.

Robert watched as the doors of the other car swung open and the three Mexicans from the White Horse Tavern got out and approached his father. He couldn't hear what they were saying, but he knew it wasn't anything good.

Through the dust, glowing in the headlights of the other car, he could see one of the Mexicans stabbing his finger in his father's chest.

Then the tallest of the three men punched his father in the face and his father fell down out of view behind the Impala.

"Fuck!" Robert shouted, his voice echoing in the emptiness of the car.

The three Mexicans in the rear view mirror stood there in the dark for a moment. Then one of them looked up at the Impala and said something to the other two.

The tall Mexican shook his head and pointed to the ground.

Then all three of them started kicking and stomping their legs.

They must be kicking the shit out him, Robert thought, desperately looking around the car for something—anything—to use as a weapon.

There was nothing in the car except his father's faded leather duffle bag on the floor next to the passenger's seat.

Robert reached down and brought it up and opened it. Inside the bag were a few books, a razor and a toothbrush, something that felt like a metal skillet, and some pens and a notebook.

He rummaged around the bag some more and at the bottom he felt something sleek and heavy. He took it out.

It was an old Army Colt .45 pistol.

Robert looked in the rear view mirror again and he could see the three Mexicans still kicking away at his father.

He felt a lurch of pure, pulverizing terror. He had never held a gun before, but as he picked up the .45 it felt strangely omnipotent in his shaking hands. It was a lot heavier than he would have ever imagined.

He opened the car door and slowly walked to the back of the Impala, the gun held high and unsteadily in his hands.

When the three Mexicans saw him they held up their hands in mock surrender and smiled.

Hell, they were practically laughing at him.

"Get away!" Robert hollered. "Get away from him. Just step the fuck back!"

The three Mexicans took a few steps backward and Robert could see his father lying in the dust bleeding. Robert bent down toward him, but kept the gun pointed up at the three Mexicans.

"You all right, Dad?"

His father muttered something unintelligible, smiled and licked the blood off his lips.

"Yeah, I'm all right," he finally said, draping his arm around the bumper. "These *bacalaos* couldn't hurt me."

"Can you stand up?" Robert asked.

His father winced as he got to his feet, spitting out a big wad of blood and staring at the three Mexicans, his eyes leveled on the tallest one.

"I told you I didn't owe you any money, Esteban," he said, his voice a mixture of rage and remorse. "Now look what you've gone and done, you stupid wetback."

The tallest one, Esteban, frowned and growled: "You a cheater, gringo! The worst kinda pig!"

"Fuck you," Dick Haywood said. "You just don't know how to play cards."

"I'll kill you, pig!" Esteban shouted.

"Take it easy," Robert said. Every nerve in his body was a steel spring, and his grip closed tightly around the .45. "No one's going to *kill* anyone. We're just going to get back in our cars and that'll be the end of it."

The one named Esteban's face glistened. A lock of oily black hair drooped over one eyebrow. His perfectly white teeth showed in a stiff grin.

"You ain't going nowhere, gringo," Esteban said, reaching in his coat pocket and taking out a long-bladed knife. "I'm gonna cut you like the pigs you are!"

Robert could feel the fear bubbling in his chest. *How the fuck did he get into this mess?* Goddamn it, he should have never let his father talk him into coming down here.

Robert held up a placatory hand. "Take it easy," he said to the tallest Mexican. "Just take it easy."

"Fuck you, gringo," Esteban said, taking a step toward him, smiling like someone possessed. "You ain't gonna shoot us. You ain't *man* enough to shoot nobody."

"Just try him, chief," Dick Haywood said, rubbing his eye and spitting blood through his teeth. "I taught my boy well. He'll put holes in you you've never even thought of. *Comprende?*"

"You're bluffing," Esteban said. Then he turned to the two other men. "He always *bluffs*. C'mon, let's cut these pigs."

Esteban moved forward and the two other Mexicans followed his lead.

"Stay where you are," Robert said, his voice trembling, the pistol bobbing in his hands like an apple in a barrel of water. "I'll shoot you if you come any closer."

Esteban smiled and slowly moved forward.

"Shoot him!" Dick Haywood shouted. "Shoot the bastard, son."

Robert looked at his father, and as he did, Esteban lunged forward, his big knife swinging wildly in the air.

"Shoot him!" Dick Haywood shouted again.

In a flash of confusion, Robert closed his eyes and pulled the trigger...

The blast was deafening.

It reverberated off the buttes and the dark open desert.

Robert thought it was just about the loudest thing he'd ever heard. Louder than the loudest backfire, louder than a tire blowing out right in front of your face.

When he opened his eyes again he saw the tall one, Esteban, lying in the dust, bleeding from a hole in his chest.

One of the other two men was now standing over Esteban. He was small, neatly put together, dark. He had a little black mustache; shiny like silk.

The man's lips twitched under his shiny little mustache. "*You killed my brother!*"

Then he bent down toward the one called Esteban and picked up the long-bladed knife.

"You killed my brother, you bastard!" he screamed again and swung the knife at Robert's face. "I'm going to kill you, *gringo!*"

Robert closed his eyes again and quickly squeezed the trigger of the .45.

He did it before he could even think.

There was a loud *Pow!*, so loud it made his ears ache.

Then he heard someone let out a painful gasp and when he opened his eyes again, he saw the man with the shiny little mustache lying in the dust next to his dead brother.

The third Mexican panicked and started running off into the ditch toward the dark buttes in the distance.

"Shoot him!" Dick Haywood shouted. "He's getting away. Shoot the motherfucker!"

But Robert didn't hear him. He was staring fixedly down at the two dead men he had just killed, lying in their own blood in the dust.

"Shoot him!" his father screamed.

But Robert couldn't move. He was frozen.

His father's voice went calm suddenly. The calm voice of murder.

"Let me have that," he said, jerking the gun out of Robert's immobile hands. "I'll do it myself."

He jumped in the ditch and fired four rounds at the shadow taking flight toward the mountains.

The echoes of the shots hung on the air and then the wind carried it toward the buttes and Robert waited and listened, with his own breathing the loudest sound in the night.

The dead men's eyes stared up at him in silent accusation. A few moments later his father came back and put his hand on Robert's shoulder, but Robert still didn't move.

"You did good, son," his father said. "I didn't think you had it in ya." He paused and looked over his shoulder toward the mountains where the third Mexican had fled. "Richie got away but he won't get far out there in the desert. I think I wounded him. He'll probably bleed to death out there, if the coyotes or snakes don't get him first."

Robert remained motionless.

He kept staring down at the two dead men. He couldn't take his eyes off them. It was like he was in a dream. He felt strangely hollow inside. Like the whole thing never happened. Like he'd never been alive before.

But it did happen and the two dead men with blood still pouring out of their motionless bodies was proof of that. It made him sick just to look at them, to try to make sense of what his eyes said he was seeing.

And then the panic rushed in. There was nothing to stop it; nothing between his own breathing and the surrounding darkness.

He *was* hollow inside. Complete emptiness filled him. It seemed to flow through him like a swarming river, taking everything inside him with it.

The strength suddenly flowed out of his legs and he slipped to the dirt on his knees in a weird kind of state of grace, like an altar boy about to take communion. His mind ran frantically over the same thought, like a gerbil on an exercise wheel: *I killed them! I killed them in cold blood. I'm a murderer. I killed them!*

His father took out of pack of cigarettes from his shirt pocket and lit one. Then he knelt down by the two dead bodies.

"Well," he said, looking over at his son, "let's finish this thing."

Chapter 8

Robert threw up, and felt the dull heat hit his cheeks. He took a deep breath of the acrid desert air and grimaced as his stomach knotted and almost betrayed him again.

He was sitting in the door of the Impala, his legs hanging out and his face in his hands. He spit out the leftover bile in his mouth and glanced up at the dim landscape, dotted here and there with clumps of sagebrush, the gray moon above throwing skeletal shadows across the slumbering cacti and hollow buttes.

About fifty yards away, he spotted two coyotes on a ridge watching him, their gray coats blending with the sand and moon and their tongues hanging out so that they seemed to be smiling mockingly at him.

Robert's father picked up the first dead Mexican—Esteban—and slung him over his shoulder and carried him to the Mexican's car. Then he came back and slung the other Mexican over his shoulder and carried him back and set him in the front seat next to his dead brother. As Robert watched this, he put his hand to his windpipe, as if he couldn't get enough air in, and turned his head sickly away.

The coyotes smiled at him one last time, then got up and slinked across the desert, one of them holding a pack rat in its mouth.

His father went around to the trunk of the Mexican's car, opened it and leaned deep into it. He took out a plastic gallon of gasoline and dipped a piece of torn fabric into the container, and then he stuck the dowsed fabric neatly inside the gas tank.

He looked up once and called out to Robert: "You might want to start up the Impala, son."

Robert turned in the seat and gripped the steering wheel. He knew that if he started the car now and drove out of here he would never be able to go back to his old life. He would never be a free man again. Never be an honest man again. Then the rest would follow: arrest and exposure, trial and sentence, separation and imprisonment.

He thought of calling the police on his cell phone. Tell them it was all just a mistake; an accident. It was self-defense. What else could he have done? They would have killed his father and probably killed him too. *Yeah, call the federales.* They'll understand. They'd have to.

But if he went to the police the local newspapers back home would find out about it. Story and pictures on page one. He would surely lose his job at the bank; they wouldn't be willing to take the bad publicity. He'd lose his job, his family's only source of income. He and Annie and the kids would be out on the streets.

Could he face that? Could he live up to it, when his children looked him in the eyes?

He told himself, *Yes;* two men were dead because of him. He wasn't going to run and hide. He'd just have to stand and pay the piper.

His conscious told him to go to the police, but his reason told him, *No;* wait and see what happens next...

He turned the key in the Impala's ignition and started it up. It roared to life like a Devil. He looked back over the seat and saw his father take out the pack of cigarettes from his shirt pocket. He watched as his father calmly lit a cigarette with his silver Zippo, then knelt down beside the gas tank and lit the doused piece of torn fabric.

It caught rather quickly and his father smiled. He ran over to the passenger's side of the Impala and got in.

"We best be getting outta here," he said coolly.

"This isn't going to work, Dad," Robert said in a little moan of a voice. "The police will know someone set that car on fire."

"So what? It'll take them a while digging around in the ashes to find the bodies. That'll buy us a little time at least." He turned once to look back at the other car. "Now, why don't we get the hell out of here."

Robert pushed down on the accelerator and drove off, looking back periodically in the rear view mirror.

It didn't happen right away, but after a few minutes he saw the other car blow; orange fire spitting up into the black night.

"*Yeeeeeee-HAW!*" his father shouted, slapping himself on the knee. "Did ya see that fucker blow? Did ya, son!"

Robert looked back in the rear view mirror. He could see the dead men in the front seat, their bodies burning up like a torch. The skin crackled and popped and turned black under the bright orange fury. Their bodies twisted from the heat. He could almost see their eyes through the crimson flames.

Robert drove on silently, the Impala lurching along through the ruts in the torturous dirt road. He had no notion now of which direction to take. He just followed the little twisting ruts.

There was nothing in sight but the buttes far off in the distance and a few dust-grayed cacti.

He tried to picture a destination. He tried to see himself being there. Somewhere. Anywhere. Arriving.

He thought of home, of Annie and the kids.

He could picture them sleeping. He missed Annie badly. He missed the sound of her voice and the look of her and the feel and smell of her. He missed his children's laughing smiles and their loving eyes. He missed them all.

He wished he could call up Annie right now and explain to her everything that happened. But he knew that was an impossibility.

He would never be able to tell her. He would never be able to tell anyone what happened out here in the desert.

He was trying to accept it now and think his way all the way through it. He had to keep his head. He couldn't let himself get in a panic about it. Nothing had changed, he told himself. No one knows what happened. No one except him and his crazy-ass father. No one could tie them to the murders. Someone might have seen them in the bar together with the Mexicans and might make the connection, but it was very unlikely. Angelina would tell no one. No one had seen them out here in the desert. He was sure of that. Everything was the same as it had always been. Everything was all right.

Everything's going to be all right, he kept telling himself, but he knew that it wasn't going to be all right. He knew sooner or later someone would find out. He was like a man carrying a bundle far heavier than he can handle but who has nonetheless found a way to raise it up and lurch forward a few steps. If his equilibrium is at all disturbed, the true weight of what he is carrying will affirm itself, and everything will come crashing down.

All he wanted to do was get back on that damn interstate. It was nowhere in sight. Total darkness enveloped them.

"Where's the highway?" he asked his father.

"Just up a spell," his father said in a remarkably calm voice. Then he pulled out the pint of whiskey from the glove box and took an easy swallow. He held it out to Robert.

"You want some?"

"No," Robert said tensely.

"It'll settle your nerves, son."

Robert shook his head nervously and kept his eyes focused on the road.

Finally he could just make out the black interstate in the distance.

A dusty black and white road sign stood in the shadows:

HWY 83.

Robert sped up and swung the car to the right, off the dirt road and onto the smooth tar of the interstate. The wheels screamed and a cloud of dust boiled up. Two of the wheels lifted for a moment and then settled.

Robert straightened the car out and drove it slowly north.

He looked over at his father.

The old man's yellow eyes were looking straight ahead as he broodingly tipped his pint again and again, sipping the mud-colored liquid carefully, running his tongue inside the bottle neck, and then around his thin lips to gather in any flavor that might have escaped him.

Chapter 9

The sun started coming up over the dashboard and the sky was a mixed painting of purple and blue. The long stretch of interstate was still deserted and the occasional roadside gas stations were all closed up this early in the morning.

Robert sat in silence in the car as it rolled like a ghost north on the divided highway. The radio was turned off, and the only other sound was the tires humming on the hot road.

He looked wearily over at his father in the passenger seat. The old man sat there, pulling on his pint and smoking all night long, and he didn't even seem tired. He had asked several times if Robert wanted him to drive, but Robert always declined. There was no way he was going to turn this car over to his father. There was no telling what might happen.

"You hungry, son?" his father finally asked, rubbing a grayish hand over his stubbled cheeks.

Despite the events of the last few hours, a tiny flame was burning in Robert's stomach.

"I could eat," he said.

He pulled off the interstate and found a little family restaurant outside of Crystal City, Texas. The big swing-sign out front said: "Ken's Place, June's Cooking."

The little roadside diner was packed with truckers, bikers, hitchhikers, and every other kind of weary southern traveler on the road to somewhere, nowhere. On the walls hung little tin signs like: "We Don't Know Where Mom Is But We Have Pop On Ice" and "If Your Wife Can't Cook Keep Her For A Pet And Eat Here."

They went in and sat at a booth by the window and Robert watched outside as the hot orange sun began climbing the desert sky like a ladder.

A skinny young blonde waitress, cute as a puppy dog with big blue eyes came over to their table and asked: "What can I get y'all?"

Her accent was so comical and heavy that Robert had a hard time understanding her, but his father apparently had no problem at all. He told the girl to bring them some of their finest chicken fried steaks and some eggs over easy, white toast, bacon, and plenty of black coffee. The blacker, the better.

The girl wrote it all down in her little tablet, smiled, and said it'd be right up.

Robert's father smiled back at her and watched her little apple ass in her little white waitress uniform wiggle as she walked away.

He let out a big wide smile, and said, "There's nothing finer in the world than a girl from Tex*ass*."

Slowly, wearily, Robert said, "This is just some big joke to you, ain't it, Dad?"

"What are you talking about now, son?"

"Everything," Robert said, a little loudly. "We just murdered a couple of guys out in the desert and you act like nothing even happened."

"Keep your fucking voice down!"

A few minutes later the cute little waitress reappeared, as if by magic, carrying a tray full of food. She set the plates down in front of them and asked if she could do anything else for them. Robert's father smiled his nasty smile and singed her with his eyes, licking his lips like a hungry coyote, all the time smiling at the young girl like she was an injured doe.

"It brings a smile to my face just to look at ya," he told her.

The girl blushed and Dick Haywood watched her ass in the little waitress uniform swish-sway across the room again.

"Goddamn that's fine!" he said, sticking a piece of bacon in his greasy mouth.

"You fucking ruined my life, you know that?" Robert said, sitting in the hot sunshine glowing in the windows. He felt hot and sick now and the food on his plate almost made his stomach tilt.

He got up and walked out of the restaurant into the desert sunshine. He lit a cigarette and paced the gravel around the car.

The sun bore down ferociously, baking the earth, spreading heat over the surface of the land. The sky was streaked with spidery white clouds that straggled across a wide wash of blue. He was submerged in it. The highway, the restaurant, the car; everything was desiccated by the desert and the heat. He was exhausted and wished he had a bed or something akin to a bed, right there where he was, a bed on which to lay his heavy, leaden head.

He could leave. Hop in the car and find the closest cop. He could. He could do it. Just leave the old man there in the diner, with his fucking chicken fried steaks and his eggs over easy and his damn greasy bacon. He could leave the old bastard there, with his old eyes raping that pretty little waitress. The old fuck deserved it. He deserved to be left out here in the middle of nowhere.

But Robert knew he couldn't leave the old man. He was still his father, after all. For better or for worse, he was still his father, even if the old bastard was just like Abraham and would probably kill his own son if had to.

Leave him!

Just leave the old fuck and go find a cop. Tell them what happened. Tell them it was self-defense and that it was all a mistake. Just a fucking big mistake.

God, he wished he could see Annie right now. She'd know what to do. He had forgotten to call her last night. She was probably worried sick. He had to talk it through with her. She'd have some ideas. Yeah, Annie would put it all in perspective.

He wasn't sure how it would all click together—it was just something he was turning around and around, a Rubik's cube of possibilities, but he knew Annie would have the solution—Annie always had the answers.

He opened the car door and searched for his cell phone. He found it in his coat pocket lying on the front seat.

"*Whatcha doing, son?*"

His father's voice came from over his shoulder like a rap on the knuckles. Cold and suspicious.

Robert dropped the phone back in his coat pocket and stood up. "I was just putting my smokes back."

"Oh," his father said, squinting his wrinkled eyes from the heavy sunshine. "I thought you might be calling Annie."

"Why would you think that?"

"Because you said you forgot to call her last night."

"Yeah, that's right," Robert said. "I better give her a call. She might be worried."

Robert grabbed his coat again and fished the cell phone out of the pocket, but his father stopped him when he started dialing.

"*What?*" Robert asked.

"I wouldn't use that if I was you, son."

"Why not?"

"The Feds can trace those little phones of yours. We don't want 'em to know we were even in this area. Why don't you just wait and call Annie from the next payphone we come across."

Robert looked up at his father. "You think the cops know it was us that killed those boys?"

"It's best to be careful, that's all. We can't give 'em anything that would make 'em think we were involved. Understand, son?"

Robert shut the phone and put it back in his coat pocket.

His father held up a doggy bag. "Here, I brought you your breakfast. You might get hungry."

They got back in the car and Robert headed it north on Highway 83.

He was more tired now than ever before in his life and he was scared and he wanted to talk to Annie badly. He glanced over at his father who was slouched in the passenger seat with a sweat-stained straw cowboy hat pulled down over his eyes. After a few minutes the old man started to snore.

Now's my chance, Robert thought. *Now's my fucking chance...!*

Chapter 10

With his long, white, nervous fingers, Texas Ranger Terry Noonan adjusted the diaphanous needle and rolled back his left shirtcuff. His eyes rested fervently on the sinewy forearm and wrist, all dotted and scarred with countless puncture-marks.

Finally, he thrust the sharp point home, pressed down the tiny piston, and sank back upon the rumpled bed, swimming in a hallucinatory globe of his own cold, precise, but admirably balanced mind.

After a few seconds, the top of Terry Noonan's head lifted off and the whole world swirled into it and he looked at the moon and stars through the window and he *was* the sky and stars, so powerful he could do anything he thought of doing.

He glanced down at the two college girls in his bed and tried to remember their names. One was a redhead with freckles on her shoulders and a fuzzy muff of kinky pink wool between her legs; the other was a bony blonde with big fat cocksucking lips and ribs that stuck out of her caramel skin like rusty railroad tracks.

Both of them were wearing brown leather riding boots, g-strings, and thigh-high leggings that were all the rage these days. Terry had picked them up after a long night of sucking down *Electric Screwdrivers* at a bar on the fringes of the UT campus in Austin and brought them to his well-furnished twelfth-story apartment on Martin Luther King Boulevard. Even though he had graduated from UT over a decade ago, he still liked living near the campus because the college girls these days were so promiscuous and the pickings were ripe and easy...like stealing fruit off a rotting tree.

The bony blonde—was her name Stacie?—was on her knees on the bed sucking Terry's cock like she was mad at it while the redhead—he'd given up trying to remember her name—was trying to stick her little pink pointy nipples in his mouth.

The rush of H had just kicked in and he was biting the tips of the redhead's nipples when his cell phone began to squawk like a baby bird crushed beneath the tires of a semi.

"Don't answer it!" the redhead moaned from above him.

The room smelled like sex and all three of them were sweating madly. All he felt was wet. His skin had turned to liquid. He was dissolving.

The phone rang a second time.

Terry let out a heavy sigh. He let go of the redhead's nipples and pushed both girls off the bed. They gave him a look like dejected puppies, and then began in on each other.

Terry reached for the phone and growled out a hello.

"Hola, Noonan," the voice on the other line said cheerfully.

The voice belonged to Randy Mueller, Senior Captain of Texas Rangers Company H. The Rangers are a division of the Texas Department of Public Safety that assists law enforcement agencies throughout the state in apprehending some of its most dangerous felons. Their history is vast and wild and includes such characters as John Coffee Hays, Ben McCulloch, and Bigfoot Wallace.

Terry grabbed a pack of Marlboros off the nightstand.

"What's all this *hola* shit, boss?" he said into the phone, wiping his sweaty long hair out of his face.

"It's Spanish," Mueller said. "It means hello."

"Since when did you start speaking Spanish?" Terry asked. He could picture Mueller on the other line: a big Teddy Roosevelt Texan with thick white hair above a shrewd, pink, irritable face and a stupid little pussy-tickler mustache.

"I got a call from the F-B-I about twenty minutes ago," Mueller said, breathing in Terry's ear so he could almost smell the scotch and Winston cigarettes on his breath. "They're down in Mexico working on a case. Do you remember a guy named Dick Haywood?"

"Yeah," Terry said, rubbing his ear and trying desperately to get the high out of his voice. "I arrested Haywood up in Bartlesville once. Theft of property and aggravated assault. Swiped some jewels off a truck. They never did find the take. What's Haywood got to do with the FBI?"

Mueller was a heavy breather. You could hear him puffing and blowing into the phone like some large and sweaty animal. "They got a couple of dead Mexicans down there," he said, *puff-puff, blow-blow.* "Poor bastards were barbequed in their car out in the desert. The Bureau thinks Dick Haywood might have something to do with it. Turns out he had a running feud with the dead spics and he was last seen arguing with them in a bar down there before they were lit up."

"What the hell was Haywood doing down in Mexico?" Terry asked.

"That's what the FBI would like to know. And they want *our* help." *Snort-snort-snort.* Likewise, *puff-puff-puff.* "More specifically they want *your* help, Noonan."

"Why me?" Terry asked.

Mueller's breath stopped. Then it started again. "Because you tracked Haywood down after that jewel heist up in Bartlesville. The feds think you can help them find him again."

Terry looked over at the girls, slithering around on the carpeted floor now like a couple of snakes. "And what did you tell them?"

"I told them you'd be on the first flight down to Ol' Mexico." Mueller said, sounding like a bull getting ready to mount Old MacDonald's cow in the back forty.

"Jesus Christ," Terry said. "I just got off a case, Mueller. I was hoping I could take some R&R. Get my head cleared a bit."

"Quit your bitching, Noonan. When the boys from the Bureau ask for a favor you give it to 'em." *Puff, snort, blow.* "Your plane leaves tomorrow morning at seven. An agent named Huddleston will meet you in Brownsville and take you to HQ. You got it?"

Terry blew frustration into the receiver. "Yeah, I got it."

"Good. Report to me when you get there."

Mueller hung up abruptly and it took Terry a while to grasp the whole situation. He was being asked—*no*—told to fly down to Mexico and help the FBI find some old bastard he arrested ten years ago? *What the fuck?*

The big bony blonde climbed back on the bed and put the heel of her leather riding boot under Terry's chin while the redhead started yanking on his cock like she was trying to pump water from a well that's run dry.

"Party's over, girls," Terry told them, rolling the blonde's legs and bony ass off his chest. "I gotta go to Mexico."

Chapter 11

Terry Noonan was met at the airport in Brownsville by a small man with big muscles. The guy was sporting trendy little spectacles with a *D* and an *H* on the side, a conservative black suit, and blonde hair that was parted ruler-straight on the left. His teeth were either capped or so perfect they were eerie. It freaked Terry out a bit. He didn't trust people with mall-bleached teeth. They reminded him of Donald Trump or that bible-thumping bastard Rick Perry.

He introduced himself as Special Agent Huddleston with the FBI, and said he was to escort Terry down to a little town in Mexico called Durango.

Huddleston pointed to a nondescript Ford and when they got in he drove with a kind of casual aggressiveness, passing cars closely and frequently. One cell-phone-using cowboy took his other hand off the wheel of his shit-covered Chevy pickup long enough to give them the finger. Huddleston seemed oblivious to all of this as he sped southward toward the border and filled Terry in on the case.

"Are you the lead investigator?" Terry asked.

"No sir," Huddleston answered in a flat and colorless voice typical of the FBI. "Agent Lopez is in charge of this one."

"Agent Lopez, huh?" Noonan cocked his eyebrows. "So they got a spic working on it?"

"A *spic,* sir?" Huddleston asked.

"Yeah, a spic," Terry answered casually. "You know, a Mexican..."

"I know what a *spic* is, sir," Huddleston said quickly.

"Then why'd you just ask me—"

Huddleston stared at Terry with an icy contempt in his gun-barrel eyes. "Lopez is one of the finest agents in the entire Bureau. Don't you ever forget that, Noonan."

They were quiet for the remainder of the ride. Terry sat in the passenger seat, staring out the window as the hot dry landscape passed them by.

Goddamn, it was hot down here, he thought bitterly. How the hell did anybody stand it? Sweating like damn pigs.

Within an hour they came to a border check, complete with U.S. Department of Homeland Security placards placed strategically and menacingly on the red and yellow arm lifts, but Huddleston passed right on through, flashing his credentials like he was the King of Siam or something.

Terry could tell in Huddleston's manner that he liked the power his badge seemed to wield. He wondered if all the FBI boys were like that. He wondered if the all-powerful Agent Lopez was going to be like that.

After they cleared the border, and another twenty minutes of sweating in the silent car, Huddleston turned off the interstate and took a ruddy little road that seemed to lead nowhere. But then again, everything out here seemed to lead nowhere.

The land they had entered was *dead.* That was the only way Terry could put it—a *deadness.* He felt like Jesus when the Spirit drove him out into the dessert for forty days, tempted by Satan and among the wild beasts, and the angels ministered to him.

He took out his handkerchief and mopped the sweat off his forehead. The goddamn air-conditioning wasn't even working. It just made the car hotter. It had to be a hundred and fifty degrees out here in the desert. And if you rolled down the windows you got a face full of dust.

"Where we going?" he asked Huddleston.

"Durango," Huddleston answered, but didn't elaborate. "I already told you that, Noonan."

"I know we're going to Durango," Terry said. "But *where* in Durango? And how much further is it?"

Huddleston looked over at this Agent Noonan, the Ranger from Austin with the big mouth and a whiner's attitude. *He'd never last a day in the FBI,* Huddleston thought resentfully.

"We're going to the local hospital," he said after a long, dry moment.

"What the hell for?" Terry asked with a smirk. "You sick?"

"One of the shooting victims got away," Huddleston said, ignoring Terry's callow sense of humor. "They brought him into the local hospital around four this morning. Agent Lopez is expecting us. Lopez wants you there during questioning of the vic." Huddleston paused, ran a thick hand over his short military-style haircut while looking in the side-mirror to make sure his government-issued shades were rightly in place. "The Bureau wants this case laid to rest as quickly as possible, Noonan. If it turns out that your guy Dick Haywood was involved in the murders, the potential's there to turn this part of the world upside down."

"Why's that?"

Huddleston raised an eyebrow. "The locals down here don't take kindly to Americans killing their own people."

Terry exhaled noisily. "What's the big deal? How many Mexicans sneak across the border every day and end up in some kind of trouble up in the States? Seems to me they shouldn't get *too* upset."

Huddleston glanced over at him. "You're not very fond of Mexicans, are you, Noonan?"

†††

They came at last to the small sun-punished town of Durango. Terry looked around. Durango seemed to be a deserted village straight out of a Peckinpah movie.

There were perhaps a dozen buildings along an unpaved street without a tree to offer contour or shade. The building at the far end on the other side might have been a school at one time, but it was boarded up. Most of the others appeared to be bars or whorehouses or some other dwelling place, but there was a depresssing lack of dwellers in Durango.

The buildings were all of clapboard, their walls gray from age and weather except for a Catholic church and a small brick adobe that served as the local town house.

"Welcome to Durango," Huddleston said.

When Terry was told he was going to Mexico he envisioned green palm trees and blue oceans and white beaches where brown beautiful Mexican girls offered him colorful margaritas.

Instead, he got *this.*

Through the dirty windshield, he could see a group of five or six shabbily-dressed Mexican boys under a pinyon tree beating a monkey with a stick. After a while, Huddleston turned the car down a narrow dusty intersection and pulled up in front of a two-story whitewashed building that Terry guessed was the hospital.

"Sure ain't the Mayo Clinic, is it?" he said.

They got out of the car and Terry followed Huddleston up to the front door. They went in and walked past the front desk and came to a flight of stairs lit by a single bead of light the size of a yellow ping-pong ball sticking out of a bare socket in the ceiling.

They climbed a flight of wooden stairs. There was a peculiar, looming trace of something in the air—very hard to identify—an unearthly sourness that stung Terry's nostrils.

They stood outside a door fronting the top-floor hall. It was the hospital administrator's office, but Terry guessed that the big shot FBI agents had taken it over. Before they went into the office, Huddleston grabbed Terry's elbow.

"Agent Lopez is waiting for us in there," he said in a low voice. "No more talk about *spics,* all right?"

Terry held out his hands and gave Huddleston a tight smile. "What is it that the Mexicans say when it's cool?"

Huddleston stared at him crookedly. "*'Sta bien?*"

"*'Sta bien,*" Terry said with that same tight smile.

They went in and were greeted by a young woman standing in the corner of the room.

Terry turned to Huddleston. "Where's Agent Lopez?" he asked, in a bewildered tone of voice.

The young woman held out her hand with the right mixture of dignity and self-assurance. A confident, good-looking woman, Terry thought.

"I'm Agent Lopez," she said, in a dead-level voice.

Terry remained still at first, his arms resting at his sides, his eyes fixed on her outstretched hand. It was a slender but sinewy hand, which made him think of a nimble little animal.

She looked at him and a smile crossed her thin brown lips. "You were expecting someone else?" she asked.

Terry took a moment before saying, "Ah...no."

He reached out and took her hand and he had to admit she had a nice grip for a woman. She held it so long that he began to feel a little embarrassed.

She's a beautiful, hard piece of work, he thought.

"Thank you for coming, Agent Noonan," Lopez said in her official tones. "The Bureau appreciates your cooperation in this matter."

Agent Mary Lopez was eyeing him up, taking stock. He had a handsome man's absence of vanity—he didn't take very good care of himself. His bottom teeth were crossed, and with his long greasy hair and his skinny face, he looked more like a drug dealer than a Texas Ranger, except for the fancy olive suit draped over his emaciated body and the expensive J.B. Hill cowboy boots that adorned his rather large feet.

"Yeah, well, I really didn't have a choice in the matter," Terry responded wearily. "I was told to come, and I came."

His face was youthful at first glance, but Lopez could tell he'd lived some lines into it. His eyes were sea-pale, full of a strange misty light, and he had long, bony fingers with ragged quicks.

"Has Agent Huddleston given you the details of the case?" Lopez asked, beginning now to pace around the small room.

Terry nodded his head as he watched her. She was wearing modest pumps and a white Calvin Klein suit and he wondered what she looked like underneath it. He liked her soft brown eyes that looked right at you as she talked, but what he noticed most about her was the bulge sticking out of her suit coat, probably made by a .32 or maybe even a .45. Big gun for such a small woman, he thought.

She walked over to a table in the middle of the room and picked up some sort of folder or card-case, flapped it up, flapped it down, and then threw it back on the table.

"One of the victims was brought in here earlier this morning," she informed Terry, her dark eyes roaming over and almost through him. "His name's Richie Montoya. Young kid, about twenty-two. He's part of a local small-time burglary and drug-running ring that fashion themselves after the *bandoleros* that rode with Pancho Villa. Not too bright either, but they live by a certain code. And they're known for not talking to the authorities. I've been waiting to question him until you got here. He doesn't have very long to live. He was shot twice in the lower back and abdomen. They could only extract one of the bullets. He's going to die, I'm afraid. Are you willing to see him?"

"Might as well," Terry said.

Lopez turned toward the door. Terry followed her out and kept sneaking peeks at her from behind as they walked down the dimly-lit hall. She had a great walk, full of female strength; erect, sheer and self-confident. Not to mention that her ass looked pretty good in that white suit.

Richie Montoya was kept in a small room in the back of the critical ward. He was lying in a bed with all kinds of tubes sticking out of him. Lopez was right; this kid didn't have very long to go. He'd probably be dead by noon.

A nun dressed in brown was sitting next to the bed with a grave look on her face. Lopez crossed the room and sat on the edge of the bed. Terry stood silently by the door, waiting to see how all this was going to play out.

Lopez touched the kid's arm gently, and said in a low voice, "Richie, I'm Agent Lopez."

The young man opened his wet eyes and nodded his head. His slender face was ashen and his thick black hair was covered in sweat. He looked around the room, smiled at Lopez, and then motioned toward Terry.

"*De dónde es él?*" His voice was low, the voice of a dead man.

"That's Special Agent Noonan," Lopez said. "He's here to help us find who did this to you." She paused and cupped Richie's hands in hers. "Can you tell me what happened to you out in the desert, Richie? Can you tell me who shot you?"

The young man looked at her and gave a wry smile. "I have no idea who shot me. I believe it was an accident."

"An accident that he hit you twice—in the back? That he killed your friends, Estebon Ruiz and his brother Raul?"

"Si," said Richie with another wry smile.

Terry let out a snort from the corner of the room. "Tell him to tell the truth; tell him he's going to die."

Lopez turned her head and gave Terry a look that said, *this is my case, stay the fuck back!*

Terry acknowledged her with a shake of the head and a heavy sigh.

Then Lopez turned back to the dying man on the bed. "You have to tell me, Richie," she said. "Just talk to me, tell me *who* shot you."

Richie's eyes shuttered. "I feel very sick and would prefer not to talk so much."

Terry's voice came alive again from the corner of the room. "Listen, Richie, I don't give a shit who shot you, but we've got to clear this thing up, you understand? Don't you want the man who shot you to be punished?"

Lopez gave Terry another callous look, but this time he ignored it. He just couldn't help it. This guy was playing her like a thrift-store mandolin.

"I never saw the man who shot me," Richie Montoya said, his smile going slightly crooked. "They shot me in the back."

"Tell us who shot the Ruiz brothers and barbequed them out in the desert," Terry said angrily.

"I don't know. Maybe the same one that shot me."

"Listen," Terry said. "This ain't the movies, Richie. You're not some *Frito Bandito.* It's all right to tell us who shot you. Suppose you don't tell who he is and he shoots somebody else. Suppose he shoots a woman or a child? It'll be on your blood, Richie. Are you prepared to take that with you to the great pearly gates?"

"That's enough, Agent Noonan," Lopez said.

"Oh, for Christ's sake. This guy thinks this is all some kind of a goddamn joke."

"I am very weak," Richie Montoya said softly. "I have much pain. I am going to die soon. I know that. But please leave now."

"We ain't leaving till we find out who shot you," Terry said.

Lopez walked over to Terry. She put her hands on her rounded hips, her eyes dark and hard. "You ain't helping this situation, Noonan," she whispered, close to his face.

Terry stared at her. She stared back, not giving him anything. Then she turned around and walked back to the bed and stood over the dying man.

"Lo siento. Simplemente relajarse. Tomalo con calma. May we come back and talk later, Richie?" she asked.

"He's going to be dead later," Terry said.

Lopez turned around and grabbed Terry by the arm and pushed him out the door. In the corridor she threw him up against the wall with more force than he thought possible out of that little body of hers.

"You're here to assist *me* in my investigation, Agent Noonan!" she yelled in a muffled, furious voice. "If you can't handle that I'll be pleased to send you back to Austin, or wherever the fuck it is you come from."

"Hey, if you think you can catch Dick Haywood by yourself, go ahead."

"I know I can catch him by myself."

"Then why don't you? Why don't you just drive me back to the States and I'll get on the first flight back to Austin."

Lopez looked up at him, her smart eyes holding his. "I'd love to do just that," she said. "But unfortunately you have something I need."

"Oh, yeah, and what's that?"

"You know Dick Haywood's tendencies. You know the essence of the man. You arrested him once and I believe you can do it again."

"You're damn right I can do it again."

She looked at him, staring, and said, "But I want you to remember that this is *my* case. I call the shots. Understood?"

Terry gave her another greasy smile. "Sure thing, boss." Then he said, "I guess we better start acting more cordial to one other, because it looks like we're in this thing together for the long haul."

Chapter 12

The phone rang four times before Annie picked up. Robert could hear her muffled yawns on the other end.

"It's me," he said.

Annie's voice came back shaggy with sleep. "Robert? What time is it?"

"I don't know," he said. "I thought you'd be up by now."

"I was still sleeping. I waited up for your call last night."

"Sorry."

In his mind's eye he saw her soft green eyes opening slowly and tiredly and wisps of her long blonde hair tangled around her shoulders.

"Robert, is everything all right?" she asked.

He was calling from a payphone at a Jenny station off the interstate. "Yeah, everything's fine."

There was a pause on the other end.

Then Annie said: "Did you pick him up?"

Robert glanced back at the car where his father was slouched in the passenger seat.

"Yeah, I picked him up."

"Where are you?"

"I don't know. I think somewhere outside Fayetville."

He stared down at his boots and pressed the heel of one boot down hard on the toe of the other. The sun was already burning the back of his neck.

Annie asked, "You'll still be back on Sunday, right?"

He paused before answering. "Yeah, I'll be home Sunday."

Inside him a voice whispered for the first time: *Tell her what happened! Tell her now!*

"You sound tired, Robert," Annie said.

He saw himself from a distance now, as though looking down from a great height.

Tell her! Tell her what happened out in the desert! You have to tell her!

"Yeah, I'm tired," he said at last. "Been driving all night. It's been over twenty-four hours since I last slept."

"Jesus, Robert, be careful." Annie's tone, although plaintive, strove to be cheerful. "I want you back in one piece, if you know what I mean."

He smiled. "I will, baby."

"I miss you."

Tell her!

"I miss you, too. How're the kids?"

"They're okay. Jack and Jenny keep asking when you'll be home. Baby Grace is cutting a tooth. Cranky as a mule."

He laughed as thoughts of his children rushed through him like a current. The smiles, the big blue eyes lighting up at the sight of him, the high-pitched laughs.

"Give them my love," he said, and a weight and a darkness fell on him.

"Robert—" Annie said slowly. "You sure you're all right?"

"Yeah, baby, I'm fine. Just tired, that's all."

"I love you."

He felt like crying.

"I love you, too."

"See you Sunday."

"Yeah. Sunday."

Chapter 13

"Tell me what you remember of Dick Haywood."

They were in Lopez's car now, heading down the dusty main street toward the White Horse Tavern where the Ruiz brothers were last seen alive.

"I busted him a few years back," Terry said, looking over at Lopez who was behind the wheel. "He served a little over two years up in Huntsville. Got out for good behavior. Same old song and dance."

"What'd he do?" Lopez asked.

"Theft of property and aggravated assault," Terry said. "Haywood hijacked a semi-trailer full of diamonds and beat up the driver pretty bad. We arrested him but they never recovered the stolen diamonds."

"Did he go quietly when you arrested him?"

"Yeah, he went quietly, but he was carrying an old Army Colt .45 when I caught up with him."

Lopez looked over at him. "Think he would've used it on you if he had the chance?"

"Don't know." Terry paused and took out a pack of cigarettes from his shirt pocket. "Mind if I light up?"

Lopez smiled. "As long as you give me one."

"You smoke?" Terry asked in a low and dismayed voice.

"Occasionally," Lopez said. "Why, does that surprise you?"

"Kind of," Terry said, handing her one. "There's a lot about you that surprises me."

"Can you light it for me?" Lopez asked.

He took out his lighter, set fire to the cigarette and held it out for her. When she leaned toward him he noticed her gun sticking out of her coat just under her left breast.

"What kind of piece you carry?" he asked.

She looked up and blew a puff of smoke out of the side of her mouth. "A SIG Sauer .380."

Terry whistled. "Big gun."

She smiled. "Big job. What do you carry?"

".50 caliber AE autoloader. What I like to call my *Grace of God.*"

"Talk about a big gun."

Terry lit a cigarette for himself. "So, tell me, Agent Lopez, why does the FBI think Dick Haywood is your shooter?"

"It's common knowledge that Haywood had a running feud with the Ruiz brothers," she said confidently. "He used to spend a lot of time down here in Durango drinking and gambling at the White Horse. Some old Mexicans saw him arguing with the Ruiz brothers and Richie Montoya the night of the murder. He's got a girlfriend by the name of Angelina Arturo who tends bar at the White Horse."

"Is that where we're going? To question his girlfriend?"

Lopez nodded her head. "I doubt she'll give us any information, but it's worth a shot."

Terry looked at her like he was trying to decide something in his mind. "Was Haywood alone that night?"

Lopez drew on her cigarette again. "Haywood was arrested the night before, up in Texas on a drunk and disorderly and driving with a suspended license. His son bailed him out and paid the fines."

"His son?" Terry asked, perplexed. "I thought all of Haywood's family were up in north Texas, on the Oklahoma border?"

"They are. But apparently the son came down to bail his old man out and take him home."

"I thought Haywood was on parole? Why'd they let him out? Getting in a bar fight must have been in conflict with the terms of his parole?"

"His parole ended two months ago. As far as we can tell, Haywood stayed clean until the bar fight."

"Did you run a check on the son? Any priors?"

"We ran him through FCIC, NCIC, and Warrant Information, but came up blank. He's married and a father of three. Just you're average ordinary citizen who appears to have gotten mixed up in a whole lot of bad shit down here."

Terry shook his head and glanced out the window at the passing landscape. Nothing but desert and saguaro. *It didn't make sense.* Why would Dick Haywood's son—a family man with a clean record—be down here in Mexico involved in a double homicide? Was it just a case of poor timing and bad luck? Sorry bastard. The poor sap probably had no idea what he had gotten himself messed up in.

"It's the paternal knot," Lopez said. "The mythological archetype. The son flees the father, hates the father, but cannot escape the tie, the loyalty. I think it was Keats who..."

"Byron," Terry said evenly. "It was Byron who got to the heart of the conflict. Keats merely lyricized."

Lopez stared at him.

"Hey, I went to college, too," Terry said, smiling.

Lopez turned the car off the road and into the gravel driveway in front of the White Horse. She cut the engine and looked over at Terry.

"This time let me do the talking, okay?"

Terry threw his cigarette out the open window. "Sure thing, *boss.*"

They got out of the car and went into the White Horse. It was dark and empty except for a few old timers sitting at the long bar, with their sweat-stained sombreros pulled down over their eyes.

"My kinda place," Terry said under his breath.

A rather large woman was slumped casually behind the bar. She had dark, almost transparent eyes with hot lights in them, like a large, pinched-faced fortune-teller.

"Are you Angelina Arturo?" Lopez asked her with no formalities.

The woman nodded her head, brooding glumly over the task of mixing herself a highball that would have floored a horse.

"*Si*. And who are you?" she said in thick, broken English.

Lopez took out her identification and flipped it on top of the scarred bar. "My name's Lopez with the Federal Bureau of Investigation. We understand you know a Dick Haywood. Is that correct?"

"Si."

"We'd like to ask you a few questions."

Angelina Arturo stared at Lopez with scorn. "You can ask, but that don't mean I'll be answering."

"We can always get a warrant."

Angelina Arturo spat on the floor. "Blah!"

"Look, we can do this easy or we can do this hard, it's your choice."

"What are you gonna do, *fresa*," Angelina said. "Shoot me with that big *cañón* you're carrying under that fancy suit of yours?"

"No," Lopez said calmly. "I'll just bring you in for obstructing justice in a federal investigation."

"You think you a big woman, huh?" Angelina said. "Carry a big gun? Do you need that big gun when you kill the men you are looking for?"

"What do you mean, *men?*" Lopez said.

She was in her element now, Terry thought.

"I misspoke," Angelina said; looking very much as if she wished her mouth had been stitched closed. "My *Englais* sometimes gets the better of me. I meant the *man* you're looking for."

"You said, men. I only asked you about Dick Haywood."

"Go fuck yourself!"

"You said, *men,* Mrs. Arturo," Lopez said, the anger coming up through her voice. "What made you say that?"

"Looking at you, you cocksucker!"

Lopez emitted a short unintentional laugh, but Terry was disgusted.

"You're talking to the FBI, lady," he said, looking at Angelina with a very bright and feverish eye. "Why don't you come out from behind that bar if you want to talk like that?"

Angelina looked at him steadily. "I suppose you know why I called her a *cocksucker,* don't ya, gringo?"

"You dirty son of a bitch!" Terry yelled.

"It's all right, Agent Noonan," Lopez said, her voice steadied now, as if she were determined to control her emotions.

Angelina stared at them both, a thin smile creeping across her fat lips. Lopez turned and stared back at her.

"Watch your back, Mrs. Arturo," she said with lethal coldness. "Because you can rest assured, I will be."

They headed toward the door and Terry heard Angelina holler at Lopez: "Watch your own back, you *cocksucker!*"

Out on the dusty parking lot Terry donned his sunglasses, took out his pack of Marlboros.

s, lit one for himself and handed them over to Lopez.

"Thanks," she said, digging eagerly into the pack.

"How do you put up with these lowlifes?" Terry said, nodding over his shoulder at the White Horse. "I don't care if she is a woman; I was about ready to punch her in the face."

Lopez smiled. "Don't you see these types working with the Rangers, Agent Noonan?"

"Sometimes," he said, sucking heavily on his cigarette. "But by the time I'm called in to investigate a case, the lowlifes are scared to death when they see me coming. I'm not bragging or anything. We don't really handle the rough stuff most of the time. We just help out the local authorities when they don't have the resources or manpower to do the job themselves. Usually it's a robbery or a missing person, occasionally we get a murder. Working for the Texas Rangers up in Austin is a lot different than working for the FBI, I guess."

"Yeah, well working for the Feds isn't all that it's cracked up to be either," Lopez said. "Most of the time it's pretty boring. It's not what you see on television or the movies."

"Most law enforcement isn't," Terry agreed. They were at the car now and he stood on the passenger's side finishing his cigarette. "Well," he said, smashing the cigarette in the dust with his boot, "what do we do now, *boss?*"

"Well, I figure Dick Haywood and that unfortunate son of his are probably already headed north as we speak. I had Agent Huddleston put out an interstate ABP on the car they were last seen in."

"What kind of car is it?" Terry asked.

"A cherry red 1966 Chevy Impala convertible," Lopez answered with a smile.

"Nice car. Every American boy's wet dream, but my guess is they've already dumped her. They'd be pretty stupid to drive around in a car like that. It'd stick out like a bloody thumb."

Lopez got in behind the wheel of the Ford and started it up. "Yeah, I know. But it's the only thing we've got to go on."

"So what do we do in the meantime?" Terry asked, settling into the passenger seat.

After a long silent while Lopez said, "I did some checking and there's one major roadway that leads all the way up to Amarillo from the border. *Highway 83.* I figure if we follow it...we just may find the Haywoods."

"What makes you think they're going back to Amarillo?"

"Robert Haywood has a wife and three kids. When you're in trouble, you go home."

"That's not where I'd go if I was in his kind of trouble." Terry flicked his cigarette out the window. "Besides, Robert Haywood might not have a say in the matter."

Chapter 14

Robert laid their wheels to the road and headed north. That was all that mattered now. Heading north; back to her, back home to Annie and the kids. He could picture them in his mind, running down the front porch to greet him when he finally made it home.

That was the problem. He kept catching himself thinking about things as if nothing had happened out here in the desert; as if those two boys hadn't been killed. Then he'd stop himself and a wave of desolation would sweep over him again.

He drove relentlessly, hardly glancing at the passing of the desert beside them. They bypassed the highway and cities like San Ygnacio, Ebanos, and Artesia Springs; staying instead on the little county roads. It was blazing hot and the shimmering dry heat made visions of water on the flat plains.

They stopped once at a Jenny station in the middle of nowhere and purchased gas, chocolate bars, ham and eggs, bread, a Styrofoam cooler, ice, beer and a couple T-bone steaks. Robert's father packed the ice, beer, and steaks into the cooler and put it in the backseat like they were on some kind of joyride. Then it was back on the road and driving for hours. They pissed standing on the side of the road, under a telephone pole with a sheet of paper nailed to it that read:

JESUS IS COMING...R U READY? On the radio they listened to an all-night Country and Western station that was playing Ernest Tubb, Johnny Cash and Hank Williams, the real Hank Williams; not that phony son of his.

After several hours of driving, dusk finally fell on the Moss Lake Pass west of Rock Springs, a lurid desert light coming from a ghostly moon between clouds and Robert knew he had gone way past the turning point. There was no turning back now. It seemed as if time had compressed somehow, like an accordion; all the years he had lived and everything that had happened to him were suddenly squeezed below the weight of what happened out here in the desert. Sure, he wanted out of this mess with the worried longing of all captive things, blindly scratching, clawing their way through a maze to the open, to the open where his only chance was, but he knew there was no getting off this hellish treadmill that had caught him up. A scared little boy had taken the place of the man he used to be; had shoved him over, grabbed the wheel and hunched forward into the dark.

It's watching me, he thought. *The road is watching me. It's got a thousand eyes. Every time I pass under a bridge or one of those huge fucking billboards with the shiny movie-star faces leering down at me, it knows it has me. It's like there's an eye hidden deep back along the road somewhere, an eye that I cannot see, keeping tabs on me, giving itself the wink.*

His eyes were weary and full of road, aching from peering too long into the dark and his back throbbed painfully and his body and mind couldn't take it anymore.

"Why don't we pull off for a while, son," his father said with a queer, indefinable little smile hovering in the hard lines around his mouth.

Slowly, reluctantly, Robert pulled the car off the county road they were on and into a deserted campground that overlooked the Wild Horse River. He drove in, switched the lights off and picked his way by moonlight, like a man who gropes his way in darkness after a light switch has been suddenly turned off.

The dirt road ended in a spot of Desert Willows blocking the wind. There were old beer cans and Coke bottles and torn discolored newspapers faintly visible on the ground.

Robert got out of the car and stretched his legs. His father looked around and immediately set about starting a fire with some chunks of pine in a pit on the shores of the river. It was a pleasant night, the cool desert air having displaced the heat of the day. Above them the sky had clouded over and the moon was hidden by a thick gray ceiling.

They sat on rocks beside the fire and his father cooked the T-bone steaks on a wire grill pushed over the flames. There was a good smell. Robert was hungry. Despite the events of the last forty-eight hours, he did not believe he had ever been hungrier.

His father went into the cooler and took out a couple of beers and handed Robert one.

"Tomorrow morning we have to get a new car," he said, sipping his beer and staring into the fire.

Robert looked up from the fire.

"Why?"

Dick Haywood laughed in a short burst that was almost a bark. "That car we're driving couldn't be more obvious, son."

"But you said nobody will be looking for us."

"That might be true, but we have to play our cards straight. Any fool with fast hands can take a tiger by the balls, but it takes a *savvy* man to keep on squeezing." His father's voice sounded strange in the darkening woods.

Robert always hated his father's snappy anecdotes. "How are we supposed to get a new car?" he asked. There was a silence before he added, "I'm not made out of money, you know? I already spent more than I can afford getting *you* out of jail. My credit card is almost at its limit."

"I plan on paying you back every red cent when we get to Amarillo. I told you that."

"And how do you plan on doing that, Dad?"

"I got a little something stashed away," his father said, his yellow pointed teeth glowing in the darkness.

"What do you mean?"

"I got a little money waiting for me up there, that's what I mean. Actually, a *lot* of money."

Robert stared at him. "Where'd you get it?" he asked suspiciously.

His father raised his eyebrows. "You don't want to know, Robert."

"What'd you do, rob a bank or something?"

His father didn't answer, just broke a stick over his knee and tossed it on the fire. Flames stole up around the driftwood, lighting the creases on the old man's thin face.

Robert stared at him. "Oh, c'mon; you're not going to tell me you robbed a bank?"

"I didn't rob no bank," his father said. "I ain't that dumb. You got to be pretty stupid to rob banks nowadays, considering the odds against you; the security, the cameras. It's virtually impossible to rob a bank these days."

"Well, where'd you get the money then?"

His father poked at the fire. "Up in Huntsville I used to hijack some semis. Me and a guy named Rocky Lapino. It was nothing big, just a small-time racket. We'd hijack the trucks and Rocky would sell the stuff we stole."

"I don't believe this, Dad," Robert said. "When did all of this happen? Was Mom still alive?"

His father was staring at the fire. "No, Mama passed on by then." He paused thoughtfully, went on: "Me and Rocky weren't making much on the scores, but then one night we hijacked a truck that was full of diamonds and expensive jewelry. It was bigger than either one of us could have dreamed. Rocky fenced the jewels and we soon parted ways. I knew the heat was on after such a big score, so I buried my half of the cash in the floor of an abandoned shack outside the Nemadji State Forest. I was arrested a week later and haven't been back yet to collect. It was enough to make a man eat his heart out to have to stand the kick and the cuff of every petty bull guard with a badge and a stick, to have nothing but oily beans and dry tortillas to eat and water to drink, when all that gorgeous money was ready for me outside, just waiting to be picked up. It might have driven me mad; but I was always a pretty stubborn one, so I just held on and bided my time. There's over a quarter million dollars just waiting for me." He looked over at his son's face glowing in the fire. "I plan on splitting it with you, son. How does that sound? A quarter of a million dollars? You and Annie won't have to worry about money for a while."

Robert put his hand to his forehead for a minute; then dragged it heavily off again. "I don't want any of your dirty money, Dad."

His father stood up and threw his empty beer can in the trees. "You're so goddamned noble, Robert, that sometimes you stink! Get the wax out of your ears, boy, and listen to what I'm telling you. I'm talking about a quarter of a million dollars, probably more..."

"I ain't interested, Dad. And neither is Annie."

His father shook his head. "You're a fool. A damned married fool. Once a man like you—with his cushy desk job and his fancy suits and ties—gets married he's absolutely bitched. Ain't got nothing no more. Nothing. Not a damn thing."

Dick Haywood turned away from his son. He shook his head and walked away from the fire across the clearing to the river. The river bank was heavy with quiet and wet from the summer rains. Beyond the river were hills. It was high and dark on both sides. Dick Haywood looked off at the horizon and the breeze stirred his hair like white smoke.

He got out a cigarette from his breast pocket and lit it, tossing the match into the fast moving waters of the river. As he stared at the fast green water he thought of something he read once in prison, something by Fenimore Cooper, the guy who wrote The Last of the Mohicans: *rivers are like human mortals, having small beginnings and ending with broad shoulders and wide mouths.*

He didn't know why he thought of that now, but he could feel his anger rise, then he held it, and spat in the river. It was a long spit and he just made it. In the weeds he saw a long green snake. It slithered along the bank of the river. It glowed and shined when the moon struck it. He couldn't bring himself to stop looking at it. He stood there and watched it, glittering, glowing, and shining.

He didn't understand that damn fool son of his. The boy got all that nobility from his mother, *God rest her soul.*

He turned and looked over his shoulder at the fire, which was bright now, just at the edge of the trees. Robert was still sitting there, all huddled up against the breeze.

After a long moment Dick Haywood stepped back and walked up the river bank into the firelight.

Robert looked up at him, not moving, realizing he was calm and in control of his emotions and this surprised him. He was tired and didn't want to lose his temper.

"You hungry?" he asked.

His father nodded his head.

Robert gave him a little smile from behind the fire. "Well, let's eat these steaks then. And why don't you go grab us a few more beers."

The steaks were delicious, eaten out in the cool of the evening, just like they used to do when Robert was young and his father would take him hunting up at the Rita Blanca Grasslands. When they finished eating the steaks, they threw the remains into the fire and watched the gristle and fat sizzle against the flames.

His father hunched over the fire and lit another cigarette. "I didn't mean to talk badly about Annie," he said with a touch of what almost sounded like reverence.

"It's okay, Dad."

"I guess I'm getting meaner in my old age," he said, staring up at the moon. "Now that I'm over a half a hundred years old, I get a little crazy sometimes." He paused and poured a swallow of beer down his throat. "We come from a strange lot, you and I. Nothing but a bunch of goddamn drunkards and loonies. Your Grandaddy; your Uncle Elmore; me, you. We all got it. It's in all of us. Melancholy and madness drips like sap down our family tree. I'm talking about the Haywood Curse, son. You know when your Uncle Elmore was younger he used to get so drunk that at the end of the week he'd go down to all the local bars and fight the biggest guy in the place. He lost a lot of those fights, but some of them he won too. He was a tough little bastard. And then there was your Grandaddy, my father. He was a binge drinker. He could go weeks without a drop, then one day he'd just fall off the edge. My mama would cry: he's at it again; he's gonna drink all our money away. You go get him, she'd say to me. You go get him out of there. I was about nine or ten years old at the time, and I'd have to go down to the local pub to try and coax him out. I'd find him belly up to the bar, drinking with all his cronies and having a good old time. Come here, kid, he'd say to me, have a Coke or RC or somethin'. Well, I couldn't never get him out of there. Then late at night I'd hear him finally come home and there'd be terrible fighting. Him and your grandma would yell and cuss and punch; terrible, awful fights. Then there was your auntie Ester. Boy, she was somethin' else. You know she had an illegitimate son?"

"Auntie Ester?" Robert said. His memories of his father's oldest sister were of a small, gray-haired lady who would visit on Thanksgiving and Christmas, her arms filled with bundles of gifts and fresh-baked butter cookies. She was so old then that after dinner she'd always fall asleep in a rocking chair still holding up a magazine in her little wrinkly hands.

"She was a real wildcat when she was young," his father said. "She wouldn't take shit from no one. *The Haywood Curse*." He paused and took another sip of beer. Then he went on, "She was about seventeen when she got pregnant and in those days, girls didn't have abortions like they do nowadays. It hurt my daddy real bad when he found out she was pregnant. He felt like he'd done his daughter wrong, that he hadn't been able to protect her from the evils of the world."

Robert thought about Annie. He knew she had had an abortion back in college, before she had met him. She hadn't told him at first, but when she did she said it was the worst thing she'd ever done. He thought about his own daughters and hoped they'd never have to go through that when they grew up.

"Your Auntie Ester had a nervous breakdown after the pregnancy," his father went on. "She had to give the kid up for adoption and that made her nuts. They gave her shock treatment, and when they gave her the juice she'd flop three feet off the table. I remember seeing it happen once. Poor girl was never the same after that. And it hurt my Daddy somethin' fierce. He took that guilt with him to his grave."

"I don't remember Grandpa that much," Robert said.

"Yeah, he died a few years after you were born. Cancer. It seems us Haywood's can't never catch a break. He worked in the metal warehouse all his life, spray-painting cars and stuff, and it just ate away at his lungs. He went to the doctor and they told him it was just a bad cold. He went back three weeks later and they told him the same thing, it was just a bad cold. *Nothing to worry about, Mr. Haywood.* Then they found the cancer in his lungs and it had spread throughout his body. I remember as a kid going to see him at the hospital down in Lubbock and he'd be drugged up on morphine, but the pain was still unbearable for him. 'Get a hammer,' he'd tell me, eyes glassy with the 'phine. 'Get a hammer and kill me, Dickie. Kill me! I can't take the pain.' I never did, but sometimes I think I should have. I should have put him out of his misery. If I would have been half a man I would have."

The night was silent. No sound but the snap of wood breaking down in the fire.

"You got to do right by your Daddy," Dick Haywood said after a moment. "No matter how much of a bastard he is. Do what he tells ya. I know your kids will do all right by you, Robert, cause you've done all right by me, son."

He lifted his head and stared for a moment. Robert watched him, but didn't say anything, as if he was poised between the present and the past.

"Well, I guess I'll hit the hay," his father said at length, standing up and stretching his long legs. "Where you gonna sleep, the front seat or the back?"

"I'll take the front," Robert said.

"All right. Good night, son."

"All right, then."

Robert watched as the old man climbed into the car, slipped his weatherworn boots off, and then disappeared behind the back seat.

Robert turned back to the fire and watched the glow when the night wind blew on it. He sipped his beer and smoked a cigarette. The night was alive with night noises now. Tree frogs croaked angrily and bats chirped away in the cypresses.

He stood up after a while and kicked dirt on the fire. Then he went over to the car and climbed into the front seat. His father was already snoring in the backseat. It had turned into a cool night but it was still warm in the car. Robert took off his jacket and draped it around him just in case it got colder.

He looked up at the sky, through the windshield, and saw a blanket of stars and the moon in the west.

Then he shut his eyes. He opened them and looked up again. There was a wind high up in the branches. He shut his eyes again and went to sleep.

Robert dreamed. He dreamed he was home. In bed. And he saw the shadows on the walls and the ceiling, cast from the big old magnolia tree outside the bedroom window.

The wind was moving the branches and there was a hunter's moon and the walls were very bright and the shadows were very dark.

The shadows looked like large, skeletal fingers, like corpse fingers.

There was something coming.

He could hear it, down the hall. Something terrible was coming. Coming for him through the shadows. He could hear it, creaking and scratching its corpse fingers along the wall.

He couldn't move. He just lay there, waiting for the Scratching Thing to get down to his room and throw open the door.

Then he realized the Scratching Thing wasn't after him at all. Or at least, not yet.

It was after Jack and Jenny and baby Grace down the hall.

Robert leapt off the bed and ran to the door and when he threw it open, he didn't see the Scratching Thing at all.

It was his father, standing in the doorway, the tree fingers moving behind him in the darkness, his face distorted with murderous delirium.

"Get away!" Robert screamed, and threw a tight fist into his father's face, a straight right to the nose, a big vicious blow, his knuckles driving through cartilage and bone, crushing it all flat.

But then in horror, Robert discovered that it wasn't his father standing in the shadowed doorway after all, but his son, Jack, now holding his ruined nose in his cuffed hands and staring up at Robert with pain and bewilderment in his eyes.

Robert woke up suddenly and violently and stared thoughtlessly into the darkness, not trying to make sense of the nightmare, only wanting it to go *away,* and some endless time later he heard his father snoring lightly in the backseat, and he realized where he was, yet there was a lingering pain left over from the dream, and he felt as if someone had stuck a flaming knife in his belly.

Chapter 15

It was after midnight when Lopez pulled the Ford into the parking lot of the Silver Spur Motel in Natalia, Texas. They had been driving for six hours straight and she was beat.

"Want to get something to eat?" Terry asked.

Lopez shook her head and a strand of that dark hair fell in her face. "Nah. I'm pretty tired. I think I'll just take a shower and hit the sack."

Terry just looked at her. She thought it was almost stupid, the way he looked at her. Sort of anxious. As though he were trying to grasp the fact that they were separating and that he would be by himself once again. Like a little kid. Something like that. But at least there wasn't any of that other stuff in it; no romantic expectations.

"Okay," he said. "See you in the morning then."

"Good night," she said.

Terry watched her as she walked to her room, her high heels clacking on the dew-stained pavement, and then she was gone, swiftly, silently, like fading light.

He crossed over the highway on foot and went to a liquor store and purchased a six-pack of Corona, a lime, and an extra pack of smokes.

He carried the beer in a brown paper sack to the motel and went behind back to the pool. He popped the top off the first beer and sat in a plastic lounge chair by the pool listening to the silence.

It was a pleasant night. A warm wind blew from the west, and heavy marshmallow clouds moved slowly across the sky, with the gray moon peeping occasionally through the rifts. He lit a cigarette and felt almost at peace.

After about fifteen minutes he cracked another beer and thought about doing a hit of H. Then the door to Lopez's room opened and she walked over to the pool. She was dressed in a big crashy white bathrobe and a starch-white motel towel draped around her head like a turban.

"I thought you were going to bed?" Terry asked.

She looked up at the sky. "It's such a nice night and I saw you out here, so I thought I'd join you."

She sat down in a chair next to him and he couldn't help noticing her crossed legs peeking through the slits in the bathrobe. They were the color of coffee with cream in them. She folded one leg over the other and dangled one of her bare feet in the air. Her toes were painted pink and they were perfect.

"Want a beer?" Terry asked.

"Love one."

He pulled a bottle out of the six-pack, opened it, cut a slice off the lime, squeezed it into the bottle and handed it to her.

She took a long sip. "That's good."

"Yeah, it is."

He lit a cigarette and handed it to her, then lighted one for himself.

"You know, Agent Lopez, I don't even know your first name."

"It's Mary."

"Mary? I would've never guessed that. You don't remind me of a Mary."

She looked at him, her face unexpectedly touched by a smile of agonized embarrassment. "What *do* I remind you of?"

He held up his head in contemplation. "Oh, I don't know, maybe a Tatiana Romanova or Honey Rider. Some spy shit like that."

She laughed and took off the towel from her head. Her hair was still wet, long and sweeping. "At least you didn't say Pussy Galore or Holly Goodhead. Nope, it's just plain old Mary. I think my father named me Mary because he wanted me to stay a virgin all my life."

Terry smiled back at her. "Where you from originally?"

"California. Modesto. Ever been there?"

"Nope," Terry said. "I haven't made it out of Texas much. My mom and dad took me to Oklahoma City once. That's about the extent of it."

Lopez sat there and rubbed at her hair with the towel. Then she looked up at him. It was the first time that she really *looked* at him—a thin, pale-looking man with long, rather greasy hair, though with a strikingly angular face and the kind of piercing brown eyes that could make you stare. He was still wearing his dark olive business suit, although his tie was undone and his collar was open.

She caught herself midstare, and glanced away.

Terry sucked on his cigarette and blew the smoke out of his nose. "So, whatever made you join the FBI?" he asked.

She was silent for a moment, thoughtful. Then she said: "Well, I went to school at Berkeley, wanted to be a writer. Studied all the great modern masters—Steinbeck, Kerouac, Hemingway. But by my senior year I knew I wanted to be something else. I wasn't a very good writer. So one day as I was walking through the commons I noticed a flyer that said the FBI was going to be on campus recruiting. The next day I went down there and signed up. Took all the tests and six months later I was on my way to Quantico. My parents objected at first. They said I was crazy, that I'd probably end up shot to death. But I stuck by my decision and as they say, the rest is history."

"How does your boyfriend feel about it?" Terry asked.

Lopez smiled. "Who said I had a boyfriend?"

"C'mon, Lopez, it's like the saying goes: God didn't make lonely girls. It isn't any of my business, but most women have boyfriends. I was just asking."

"I don't know what most women have," she said, a little defensively. "The men I usually meet can't handle the fact that I work for the FBI. They feel threatened by it. I don't know why. I guess they don't like the idea of their girlfriend carrying a loaded gun around. And the hours aren't the best. This line of work isn't very conducive to relationships."

"Yeah, I know what you mean," Terry said, sucking on his cigarette. "It's funny, when I was a kid growing up I used to hate cops. Me and the other kids in the neighborhood, we used to always be getting in trouble, always getting rousted by the cops. I suppose if we had guns like the gangs do nowadays, I'd have shot every cop in sight. Parents never seem to care. Teachers, they forgot how to care, but as you grow a little older you begin to realize what cops are all about. They're just doing their job, enforcing the law, and raising families. If you break the law, you do the time. That's about all there is to it. I learned to respect that. I even began to realize that cops are just about the only people left that stand for something. So when I got out of college, I joined up. I had big dreams. Huh..."

Lopez stared at him. "Do you have someone back home in Austin?"

Terry thought about it, sipping his beer. "Nah. I was married once, but that didn't work out."

"Any kids?"

He laughed. "No kids."

Lopez finished her beer and looked up at the leaden dark night again.

"Well, I better hit the sack," she said, standing up.

"Want another beer first?"

She shook her head, and her dark hair danced over her shoulders. "No thanks, I'm beat. I'm already up past my bedtime."

She walked past him and let her hand trail over his shoulder lightly. "It was nice talking with you, Noonan."

"My pleasure, Lopez."

"See you in the morning," she said, yawning. "Don't stay up too late. We've got a lot of work to do. Got a lot of driving ahead of us tomorrow morning."

He watched her as she walked away toward her room. She looked back once and waved, and he felt something weird but pleasant in his stomach, like he used to feel back in high school whenever he got up enough courage to talk to a pretty girl. And his heart started racing for some reason, like he had something to be guilty about.

He waved back and when Lopez went into her room he leaned his head back on the plastic pool chair and inhaled on his cigarette. He blew the smoke up at the moon shining in the west and sighed. Then he shut his eyes. He opened them and looked up again. There was a wind high up in the pecan trees.

Chapter 16

Robert woke stiff and cramped. He raised his head and looked in the back seat of the car but his father wasn't there.

A flicker of panic swept through him like a cold, clear gust of wind and he sat up quickly.

He looked out the fogged windshield.

His father was hunched over the smoldering fire.

Robert climbed out of the car and sniffed the smells of the cool earth and found he wasn't sleepy any more.

A morning breeze was blowing and it had a pleasant salty tang. The sun had risen a little higher, mottled red above the hills, and it was already beginning to warm the back of his neck. He walked over to the fire.

"Good morning, son," his father said. "You sleep all right?"

"Yeah, fine."

"You hungry?"

"Hungry as hell."

Into a skillet his father was laying slices of ham, and as the skillet grew hot and the greases spit, he turned the ham and broke four eggs into the hot skillet.

"Why don't you go get the bread out of my bag," his father said, kneeling over the fire.

Robert turned from the open fire and walked back to the car. In the back seat he opened his father's duffle bag and took out a loaf of bread. Then he walked back to the fire and gave the loaf of bread to his father.

"Thanks, son," his father said.

"Where's the gun?" Robert said, his voice low and harsh.

"What?" his father asked, looking up at him from his kneeling position.

"The gun," Robert said. "It wasn't in your bag. Where is it?"

His father stood up and lifted the bottom of his shirt with a bright, cheerful, and utterly predatory smile, revealing the old Army Colt .45 stuck in the waistband of his jeans.

"What are you planning on doing with it?" Robert asked.

"Whatta mean, son?"

"Why you carrying that gun around, that's what I mean."

"I just feel more comfortable with it. In case we need it. That's all. Geez, son, take it easy, you're all jumpy this morning."

He knelt back over the fire and flipped the eggs on the skillet.

"I just want to know what you think you'll need it for," Robert said, staring down at him.

"Relax, son," his father said. "If it makes you feel better, I'll put the gun back in my bag after we eat." He took three or four slices of bread and set them by the fire. "Do you like to dip your bread in the ham fat or do you like it like a sandwich?"

"Sandwich," Robert said.

"Me, too," his father said, picking up a slice of ham and laying it on one of the pieces of bread, then he slid an egg on top of it.

Robert took the sandwich and started eating. The hot fried ham and egg tasted wonderful. His father made himself a sandwich and sat back on a rock to eat it. When he was done he lighted a cigarette, smoked it for about five seconds, then stood up and kicked dirt on the fire.

"Well," he said, stretching his legs, "we best get going."

Robert finished his own sandwich and followed his father back toward the car. His father leaned in and took out the duffle bag and slung it over his shoulder. Then he turned toward the dirt road and started walking away.

"Where you going?" Robert called after him.

"I told you last night, we got to get ourselves a new vehicle."

Robert ran after him. "What? You just plan on leaving your car here?"

His father stopped and looked back at the Impala. Then he squinted his eyes, and said, "Sure is hard leaving her like that. She's such a lovely old thing and pure hickory through and through. She was better than most women I've known." He paused for a moment. "She sticks out, son. She sticks out like an easy chair in the middle of a battlefield."

"What are we going to do? Walk back to Amarillo?"

His father laughed. "I reckon Annie wouldn't be too pleased with that, us showing up a couple weeks from now."

"This ain't funny, Dad," Robert said. "I want to know how you plan on getting us home without a damn car. I sure as hell don't have the money to buy another one."

"I don't plan on *buying* one, son."

Robert could not keep his voice steady. "I ain't gonna steal a car, Dad. I've never stole anything in my whole life."

"It's our only option, Robert."

"Why can't we just keep your car?"

"Jesus, boy! Do you ever listen to a goddamn thing that's told to ya? We can't be driving around in that. The police will spot us for sure."

"But you said—"

"We've got to be careful, son. Right now we're just a tree in a landscape of millions. But we've got to keep it that way. Let 'em find that one tree. The odds are in our favor they won't."

"You don't think stealing someone's car is going to attract attention?"

"Hell, by the time the cops get around to looking into a stolen vehicle report, we'll already have ditched it up in Amarillo."

Robert felt like he was standing at another crossroads; like walking a tight-rope without a balancing pole and with no net under him. All he wanted to do was get back home, to Annie and the kids.

"But I don't want to take someone's car," he said, almost to himself.

His father flashed that smile of his. "Hell, we've done worse, son."

"That ain't fucking funny, Dad. I ain't laughing."

"Listen, we won't take anything fancy. Hell, the guy will probably thank us after he gets the insurance check. It's the only way, Robert. Don't you see?"

Robert's reluctance to follow his father was plainly visible on his face, but his father ignored it. He turned and started walking down the dirt road again.

"You coming or not?" he called out over his shoulder.

Robert stared at the ground beneath his feet. It was like being lost in the darkest heart of some impenetrable forest and seeing a way out, but for now he remains in darkness. Shaking his head, he ran to catch up to his father.

Chapter 17

They were crouched down in a clump of trees that overlooked the Rolling Ridge Trailer Park on the outskirts of Eagle Pass. Robert's father had a cigarette dangling from the corner of his mouth and the smoke was getting in Robert's eyes.

"Which one do you like, son?" his father asked, eyeing up the cars parked in a neat little row next to the mobile homes.

"You choose," Robert said. He still didn't like the idea of stealing someone's car. He didn't like it; still and all, he just didn't like it.

"How about that one?" his father said, pointing at a black and gold Trans Am that looked like the car in *Smokey and the Bandit.*

"Too flashy," Robert said.

"Yeah, you're right." His father narrowed his eyes and scanned the parked cars like he was window shopping at Macy's. "How about that one?"

It was a rusted-out Chevy pick-up with a sticker on its rear bumper that read: PASS WITH CARE...DRIVER CHEWING TOBACCO and a couple of empty beer cans lying in the bed.

"Whatta ya think, son?"

"I don't care," Robert said, shaking his head.

His father smiled. "It's perfect. The person that owns that thing is probably still sleeping off last night's drunk. When they eventually realize their car's not here, first thing they'll ask themselves is 'Now, did I really drive home last night?' By the time they figure out the car is stolen we'll already be in Amarillo." He chuckled like he'd just told the funniest joke that mankind had ever heard.

"Just hurry up, all right," Robert said.

"What, you're not coming?"

"I'll wait here."

His father shrugged his shoulders. "Suit yourself."

"Just be careful," Robert said, almost as an afterthought.

His father snuck out of the clump of trees, keeping low the whole time, and walked over behind the Chevy. It was a Silverado, rusted along its baseboards and a right headlamp with a spiderweb of cracks over its entirety. He ran his palm over the back side and up to the door, like he was stroking a woman. The door was unlocked so he slid in behind the wheel. Robert lost sight of him for a few seconds as he leaned down in the seat to hotwire the engine.

It tried turning over once, then a second time, but didn't catch. On the third try she roared to life and Robert saw his dad's white head pop back up and he had a big shit-eating smile on his face, the cigarette still dangling from the side of his lips.

The truck backed up slowly, turned around, and then drove up to the clump of trees. Robert went up to the passenger's side door and stuck his head in.

"I'm driving, Dad," he said. "So move over."

"Hell no," his father said, shaking his head. "I stole it, I drive it. If you want to drive so bad, you steal your own damn truck."

Robert paused a moment, and thought about doing just that, letting the old man drive off by himself. It would be a good riddance to see him go.

But then what?

"You coming?" his father said, revving up the engine.
Robert slid into the passenger seat and shut the door. His father smiled over at him, gave the truck some gas, then tore out of there.

Chapter 18

Terry Noonan woke up before the sun. The room was dark, shaded by brown plastic curtains. It was small, but decent enough for a roadside motel room.

He slowly got out of bed and opened the curtains and stood at the window looking out. A semi raced by on the interstate and the horizon was just starting to turn pink. Outside in the gravel lot the heat was already up. It must have rained all night. Now it was steaming with that heady aroma of drenched pavement under a hot morning sun. He wondered if Lopez was awake yet.

Yawning, he went into the bathroom and turned on the shower, nice and hot. The steam filled the room and Terry stepped under the hot water and let his body relax. He felt good. That little chat with Lopez by the pool last night made him feel good. He felt better than he had in a long, long time.

After the shower he dried off and put on a new suit, a dark Armani, one of his favorites. Then he slipped his feet into some silk socks and his expensive J.B. Hills. Smiling, he opened the door and stepped into the warm sunshine and walked across the parking lot to a pancake restaurant on the other side of the highway.

Lopez was waiting for him in a booth by a window. Her suit was yellow today, her dark hair tied into a long ponytail. She smiled when she saw him and nodded at his expensive suit.

"You look nice today," she said, her little pointer teeth showing a faint touch of road-weary yellow in the artificial brightness of the restaurant.

"What? This?" Terry said. "It's just something I threw on."

He smiled down at her and slid into the faux-leather booth.

"You always dress like that when you're working a case?" she asked.

He shrugged. "Good suits are my *one* luxury."

He took out his pack of cigarettes and offered her one.

"No thank you," she said. "I don't like to smoke until I've got something in my belly."

Terry lit one for himself. Then he turned his head and looked at the crowd; a hopelessly stymied milieu of farmers, truckers, and other assorted Texas dingbats.

The place was packed and very loud. There were three waitresses working the joint and an oversized ape doing the cooking behind the counter.

Just as he got his cigarette going one of the waitresses came rushing over to the table. She was long past her expiration date with greasy gray hair and an overworked frown.

"I'm sorry, sir," she said, "but you can't smoke that in here."

Terry winced and looked at her name tag which read: "Alice."

"Well, *Alice,*" he said, "is there a smoking section you might be able to move us to?"

Alice shook her head. "No, sir, the entire restaurant is *smoke-free.*"

"Jesus," Terry said, putting the cigarette out on a saucer. "It's getting to be that a man can't smoke anywhere in Texas nowadays. Last time I checked these things were still legal."

"I'm sorry, sir," Alice said, swiping a strand of greasy hair behind her ear. "Would you like to order now?"

Terry picked up a menu. "I'll take a large coffee, black, a large orange juice, a large RC Cola, the All-American breakfast and an extra side of bacon."

Alice wrote it all down on her pad then turned to Lopez. "What can I get you, honey?"

"A bagel with cream cheese and some coffee, thank you," Lopez said.

The waitress took the menus and walked away.

"You don't eat much," Terry said to Lopez.

He thought she was blushing but he couldn't tell for sure.

"I was thinking," he said, "what if you're wrong about Dick Haywood?"

"What do you mean?"

"Well, what do we really have to go on?" Terry said. "I mean, the woman at that bar in Mexico didn't give us anything and Richie Montoya sure ain't talking. What if Dick Haywood isn't our guy?"

"He's got to be," Lopez said. "Haywood had a running feud with the Ruiz brothers and we have witnesses that say they saw Haywood in the bar that night arguing with them."

"What witnesses? A few old drunk Mexicans that were too shit-faced to notice anything?"

Lopez looked up at him and shuffled in the booth. "Agent Huddleston called me this morning. We got the results back from FOI."

Terry sighed, a look on his emaciated face that said he'd rather be anywhere else than stuck in some roadside shithole diner on the edge of nowhere.

"Everything is acronyms these days. Please, Lopez, be so kind to tell me what the hell *FOI* means."

"The Federal Office of Intelligence. Maybe the only good thing George Bush did the whole time he was in the White House. It's made up of computer banks that serve as a central clearing-house for law-enforcement agencies and the computer geeks who run them. We can access the fingerprints of almost anyone in America convicted of a felony crime since 1989 or so. The FOI also supplies ballistic reports for comparison, blood-typing on felons when available, voice-prints, and computer-generated pictures of suspected criminals. The FOI is saying that the Ruiz brothers were definitely shot with a .45 and I've done my research on Dick Haywood. He carries a .45."

"A lot of people carry .45's," Terry said. "Especially in Texas. That doesn't prove anything. Have you tried making contact with Haywood? Have you contacted his son's wife?"

"No. We're waiting until we have something more substantial. We don't want to scare Haywood off. Right now, he doesn't know we're looking for him. That's to our advantage. FOI ran Robert Haywood's phone records and he called home once since bailing his father out of jail. We'll wait and see what happens next."

"Well, what if something else goes down in the meantime?"

"Like what?"

"What if Dick Haywood kills someone while we're waiting."

"That's a chance we have to take right now," Lopez said. "Dick Haywood has a long history of robbery and aggravated assault, but as far as we know he's never killed anyone before this."

Terry looked out the window at the long stretch of highway. "I was just last week reading this story by D.H. Lawrence—you know, the guy who wrote *Lady Chatterly's Lover*—where he says..."

Lopez held up her hand. "Wait a minute. *Lady Chatterly's Lover?*"

Terry shrugged. "Great book. Full of sex and violence. The way any good book should be. Anyway, Lawrence says the typical American male is private, independent, and sort of a natural born killer, in his heart."

Lopez used her thumb to rub the lid above her right eye. "We're hoping what happened with the Ruiz's was just a freak accident. Self-defense or something. But by starting the Ruiz's car on fire and destroying evidence, Dick Haywood has upped the ante. Wouldn't you agree, Noonan?"

The waitress came back to the table and poured their coffee. Lopez put cream and sugar in hers and Terry took it black.

"And Robert Haywood?" he asked when the waitress left their table again. "What's his role in all this?"

"Like I said before, as far as we can tell Robert Haywood is just a law-abiding family man who was in the wrong place at the wrong time. But until we find him we won't know for sure. The first step is finding him. We think they're heading back home to Amarillo so we've set up roadblocks all along the Highway 83 corridor."

"What if they take the back roads?"

"There's always that possibility. That's why we don't want to make contact with Robert's wife. We don't want them to know we're looking for them. We'll continue to keep a trace on Robert's phone, try to track them down. Hopefully they haven't got rid of the gun yet. Then if we pick them up we can match it with the slugs taken out of the Ruiz brothers and Richie Montoya."

Terry blew the hot out of his coffee. "Sounds like a long shot to me."

"Yeah, but it's the only shot we've got so far," Lopez said with a shrug.

The waitress brought them their food and Terry proceeded to devour his. When he was finished he stood up and excused himself.

"I'll be back in a minute," he said.

Next to the cash register, held by the bottle of catsup and the white mustard jar, was a folded newspaper. Terry reached for it, picked out the sports page, and walked across the restaurant to the men's room. He opened one of the stalls, took out a Ziploc sandwich bag containing three rolled joints, lit one of them, and sat down to read the sports page.

A few seconds later there was a rather peremptory knocking at the door. At first Terry thought it was Alice tracking him down to remind him that the entire restaurant was *smoke-free, sir.*

He ignored the knocking, took another drag on his joint, and went back to reading the sports page: *The Astros had just lost their seventh straight.*

A voice came through hollowly from the other side:

"Noonan! You in there?"

It was Lopez.

Terry flushed the joint and popped an Ice Breaker in his mouth. "Yeah, what is it?"

"They found the car," Lopez said. "They found Dick Haywood's car."

When Terry opened the door Lopez was standing there with a big anxious smile on her face.

"Where they'd find it?" he asked her.

"It was abandoned in some campground east of Eagle Pass. We've got to get up there as quickly as we can. We have a chopper waiting for us at Fort McMullen."

"A chopper?" Terry asked with a nervous twinge in his voice.

Lopez nodded her head excitedly. "Yeah, a helicopter. C'mon, we've got to go."

The chopper was waiting for them on the runway at Fort McMullen. It was one of those big green Army things with a gold star and DEATH FROM ABOVE painted on its nose and a Playboy bunny on its tail.

Lopez parked the Taurus and grabbed her bag out of the backseat, but Terry hadn't moved.

"What's wrong?" she asked.

Terry looked over at her. His face was racked with nerves.

"What is it?" Lopez asked again.

Terry ran a distracted hand through his long hair. "I've never been on one of those things," he said, nodding at the big, green whirlybird.

"What? You mean to tell me you're afraid of flying?"

"I ain't afraid of flying," Terry said. "But in a helicopter?"

"C'mon, there's nothing to worry about," Lopez said, grabbing Noonan's bag out of the back seat. "Just keep your head down when you approach the main rotor blades."

"Why?" Terry asked, stepping slowly out of the car.

"Because if a stiff breeze hits just right, it might chop your head off."

"Wonderful."

Lopez handed him his bag. Then she made a dash toward the chopper. Terry swore under his breath and reluctantly followed her, keeping his head down the whole way.

A tall, slender soldier in desert fatigues was waiting for them on the chopper. He had an unlit *Sancho Panza* cigar dangling from the corner of his mouth, wearing a helmet that had "KILL" inscribed on the side of it.

"You Lopez?" he called out over the din of the engine.

"Yep."

"Hop on then," the soldier said, holding out his hand for her. "I'm Major Oates. I've got orders to drop you down on the Wild Horse. That right?"

"Yeah, that's right," Lopez said.

Oates helped her on and strapped her into a seat. Then he turned to Terry who was bending so low that he looked like he was having a bowel movement right there on the tarmac.

"You coming?" Oates asked, holding out his hand.

Terry reached out and Oates heaved him onto the chopper.

"Okay, you'll need to put these on," Oates said, handing them each a pair of helmets.

"What do we need these for?" Terry shouted above the hiss of wind through the rotors.

Oates smiled a toothy grin. "In case the engines stall out."

Terry's frown deepened. "Wonderful."

At liftoff, he said a Hail Mary, even though he never considered himself a deeply religious man. He was curled into a seat opposite Lopez, the knees of his long legs up to his shoulders. She was sitting there with a big smile on her face. The sudden swell of the revving engine made the earth tremble and Terry's face went milk-white.

"Relax," Lopez told him, but he could barely hear her over the noise of the chopper's engines.

Then the chopper launched, and Terry felt a sinking in his gut. He looked out the window and saw that they'd parted ways with the earth, lifting off from the tarmac into an embracing blue vista of sky.

He kept his eyes off into the distance as the heavy blades of the helicopter cut through the wind like a demented, laughing devil.

The landscape below looked like a map, beige and green and it was all rather beautiful, as long as he didn't think about what would happen if the engines stalled out.

Chapter 19

The chopper set them down outside the small town of Eagle Pass, where another government-issued Ford was waiting for them.

It was only about a ten minute drive to the campground overlooking the Wild Horse River. When they pulled in they could see the Texas Highway Patrol cars surrounding the area.

Lopez parked the car and they got out and walked quickly over to Dick Haywood's abandoned red Impala. It was parked under a shade of trees by the river. Cordoned off with yellow crime-scene tape, blocked off in a wide circle with only one way in and one way out and some State Bears were standing around the Impala like it was a prized trophy bass.

One of the troopers, wearing a Smokey the Bear hat came up to Terry. "You from the FBI?" he asked.

Terry shook his head and pointed at Lopez. "Nope; but she is."

The man in the trooper hat looked at Lopez and his eyes deepened in his head. He tipped his sunglasses down to get a better look at her. Then he brought one of his large hairy hands up to his face and wiped the sweat off.

"Are you Special Agent Lopez?" he asked. "I was told to keep this area secure until you arrived."

Lopez kept her eyes on the Impala. "Has anyone touched the car?"

"No, sir—I mean, no ma'am."

Terry let out a chuckle but Lopez wasn't laughing.

"You sure no one has touched it yet?" she asked, all business.

The trooper nodded his head vigorously and the sweat flew off his forehead. "I called you guys as soon as one of my boys found it," he said, pointing his big slab of a hand at another trooper. "Metcalf there was the first to come across it."

Lopez turned to the younger trooper. He looked like he was barely eighteen.

"When did you find the car?" she asked.

"About nine this morning, give or take," Metcalf said. He widened his mouth and showed her a space between two of his teeth. It was probably supposed to be a grin. "I remembered there was an APB out on it. The reason I remember is I always wanted a sweet-ass car like—"

Lopez cut him short. "I need this car swept for trace hairs and fibers. A forensic team in little *white bunny suits* from the Bureau should be arriving later this afternoon with USB microscopes and evidence vacuums. Until then, no one but me touches this car. Is that understood?"

The two troopers, the old and fat one and the young and skinny one, nodded their heads simultaneously. They looked strangely like Laurel and Hardy.

Lopez went up behind the door of the Impala and looked in the window.

The car was clean. Nothing was left behind.

Then she went around the front of the car to the passenger's side.

She pulled out a pair of latex gloves from the inside pocket of her yellow suit coat and for the next ten minutes she dusted the car with a fine white powder that showed prints off the door handles, the headrest, the windows, the radio, and the steering wheel, and pretty soon it looked as if someone had gone crazy with a bottle of talcum powder.

"Shouldn't we wait for that forensic team in little white bunny suits?" Terry asked.

Lopez smiled up at him. "I'm not an *all-science* kind of gal, Noonan. Sometimes I can be as *old-fashioned* as the rest of 'em."

When she finally climbed out of the car, she told the fat trooper, "We'll need to clear this area. No one comes within a hundred yards of this car, understood? I need to have foot casts around the area done immediately before the footprint evidence is completely obliterated."

Terry was watching all this with something close to awe. Lopez really knew what she was doing and she wasn't about to let the State Bears get in her way. She had a job to do and she was doing it. And she was damn sexy doing it, too.

She snapped off the latex gloves and scanned the area. Then she walked over to where Terry was standing.

"This is it, Noonan," she said, squinting off into the fading horizon. "This is our big break."

"Whatta mean?" he asked, ridging his forehead at her.

"This is most definitely Dick Haywood's car," she went on, smiling. She flung her hands encouragingly wide, to impress it on him. "Abandoned right off *Highway 83,* just like I thought. They're bound to show up at the next roadblock."

"What if they don't?" Terry said hesitantly. "What if they decide to stay off the main interstates? We don't even know what kind of vehicle they're driving now."

"I've put a trace on Robert Haywood's credit card," Lopez said, smiling smugly. "If they try to rent a car, we'll know about it."

Terry said, "I don't think Dick Haywood is the Avis type of guy, Lopez. My guess is that they're going to—or they already have—stolen another vehicle."

Lopez nodded her head. "Yeah, I already thought of that. I told Agent Huddleston to contact me if he gets any reports of grand theft in the area." She paused now and smiled at him. "This is it, Noonan; we've got them on the run now."

Terry smiled back at her. "Whatta think? Should we make contact with them yet?"

"Not yet," Lopez said. "I don't want to give away our hand. Let's just wait and see what the roadblocks turn up…"

Chapter 20

They were stopped at a crossroads out in the middle of nowhere. The sun was up high and burning down on top of them. The wind was blowing dust from the side of the road and crickets were chirping in the high yellow grass.

Dick Haywood kept his hands on the steering wheel and looked both ways.

"You still got that road atlas?" he asked.

Robert nodded his head. "Yeah, I still got it. But why do you need it? The sign back there said Highway 83 is straight up ahead."

His father wrinkled his nose, squinted down it with an air of deep concentration.

"I'm thinking about taking a different way, son."

"What? Why?" Robert asked, looking mildly surprised and rather annoyed.

"83's too crowded," his father said.

"But it's a straight shot right up to Amarillo."

"I like to take the scenic route," his father said, winking. "Now let me have a look at that damn atlas."

Robert turned and reached over the front seat and took out the atlas from his bag in the back. He handed it to his father and his father turned the pages and squinted his eyes.

"Here we go," he said after a moment. "There's a little by-way called 60. A one-lane highway that cuts right through the Buckhorn Draw, hugs the borders of San Angelo and Sweetwater, and slips right into Amarillo. If we move we can be home by tomorrow night and you can see that pretty little wife of yours again, son."

A sudden wave of exuberance shot through Robert like an electric shock. "Well, where do we pick up this Highway 60?" He wanted nothing more than to get back home, to the safety and security of Annie and the kids. He was so tired of everything; so tired of this fucking nightmare. So damn tired.

His father studied the map, then leaned an arm out the side of the Silverado, and looked across at the calm, blue horizon.

"Looks like it's about fifteen miles east on 70. Highway 60 intersects it right outside a town called Barksdale."

He took his foot off the brake and turned the car east on 70. The road was deserted. The wind knocked against the car and Robert felt sleepy sitting in the passenger seat. The sun was shining down on him pleasantly and he started thinking about home. He couldn't wait to see Annie and the kids. He wondered what they were doing right now. He could almost picture them behind his eyes...Annie smiling her inviting smile and pushing her blonde hair out of her face, the kids running around the driveway laughing and playing...

He must have fallen asleep, because when he opened his eyes again the sun had moved higher in the sky and the clouds had started to mushroom.

"What time is it?" he asked his father.

"It's about noon," Dick Haywood said, gripping the steering wheel and smoking a cigarette. "You want to stop somewhere and get a bite to eat?"

"Nah, I ain't hungry."

His father shook his sinewy shoulders. "Suit yourself. I can keep going for a couple more hours or so. Then I got to eat."

"That's fine," Robert said sleepily.

He closed his eyes and started thinking about Annie and the kids again.

Chapter 21

By noon the roadblocks had turned up nothing.

Terry and Lopez were sitting out on Highway 83, on the outskirts of Leakey, Texas. It was a beautiful, warm summer day. The sun was shining and the birds were tweedle-lee-deeing, but Lopez's mood was tempered by the fact that her roadblocks were proving fruitless. Members of the Texas State Police and Highway Patrol were stopping a lot of cars, but no one was matching the description of Robert and Dick Haywood.

It was a waiting game. She knew it was a waiting game. A long and boring waiting game.

Terry was passing the time by playing solitaire on the hood of the Taurus. Lopez kept getting up anxiously and walking around, staring off at all the stopped cars out on the roadblock.

"You hungry?" Terry asked. "We could call in some food."

"Nope," Lopez said, squinting her eyes into the sun.

"We gotta eat," Terry urged.

"If you're hungry, order something. I ain't hungry."

Terry flipped a card. "We could be out here all day and all night, you know that, don't you?"

Lopez ignored him. Her cell phone rang and she grabbed it out of her inside coat pocket.

"Lopez," she said into it. Then she nodded her head slowly. "Yeah? Okay. Good. Good. Thank you, Huddleston."

She hung up the phone and stuck it quickly back inside her coat.

"What's up?" Terry asked, lifting his chin.

"We got a report of a stolen vehicle," she said, a certain yearning wistfulness in her eyes.

"Where?"

"At a place called the Rolling Ridge Trailer Park, outside Rock Springs."

Terry threw his cigarette into the sagebrush and walked around the car and pulled out a map from the glove box.

Lopez almost grimaced at the site of the map. "I got a GPS that can—"

Terry cut her off. "Picasso once said, 'Computers are completely uninteresting—all they can do is spew out answers.' I told you I like to do things the old-fashioned way."

He spread the map across the trunk of the car and Lopez stood next to him, looking over his shoulder. Her perfume smelled sweet, like a mango cream pie.

"Here it is," he said, punching his finger at the map. "The trailer park is right off *Highway 83.*"

Lopez paused and glanced up again at the cars out on the roadblock. "I don't get it," she said. "They should have been here by now. Are there any other routes out of Rock Springs other than 83?"

"Just this road here," Terry said, staring down intently at the map. "But it's just a one-laner called 60. Maybe they took that instead."

She looked up at him. "You think so?"

He shrugged his shoulders. "They'd probably want to keep off the main interstate if they could."

Lopez folded the map and handed it back to Terry.

"Okay," she said. "We have the make and license of the vehicle that was stolen. It's a 1999 Chevy Silverado with Texas plates. We'll put out an all-states APB and concentrate our roadblocks up on Highway 60. Maybe we can send up some air surveillance, too." She rubbed her nose and paused and looked off into the distance again. "If they are on Highway 60; we'll find 'em. It's only a matter of time."

Chapter 22

They were making good time now. The old V8 Silverado could still really move, hitting a top speed of a hundred and ten at one point.

The dry landscape whizzed by—telephone poles, cacti, enchilada joints, fruit stands; austral wisdom on the obsolescent billboard signs:

DRINK SHINER BOCK; TEXAS: LOVE IT OR RELOCATE; VISIT SUTTON COUNTY'S ONLY REAL LIVE SNAKEPIT!

They had the windows rolled down and the breeze blowing in felt good.

Dick Haywood was gripping the steering wheel like a man possessed. He pushed the gas on straight-aways and took turns at an amazing speed; tightly, like he was an old NASCAR driver from the Fifties.

They zoomed through the Buckhorn Draw without seeing another soul on Highway 60. The roads leading into the Draw were narrow and lined with tall cottonwood trees.

They stopped for gas at a small Jenny station in Hutchinson, bought a bunch of fruit from a stand outside Fowler, and by the time the sun had once again lost its daily battle and evening started its slow descent, they had passed out of the Draw and into the town of San Angelo...

†††

It was well into the evening before Lopez was able to pull enough local strings to get the roadblock set up on Highway 60, on both ends of the Buckhorn Draw, from Hutchinson to San Angelo. She was furious that it didn't get done quicker and she had her doubts that they would find the Haywoods here. Instead, she was staking her bets on the roadblock that Agent Huddleston set up much farther north, between Sweetwater and Lubbock.

She was exhausted and starving from driving all day and she knew that her and Noonan needed some rest and some food in their bellies.

They rented a couple rooms at the Holiday Inn in Lake Gardens and grabbed a bite to eat at a rather fancy steak place at the intersection of Highway 60 and Deadwood Canyon.

Terry ordered a couple tall beers and Lopez ordered them both a porterhouse, homemade slaw, Texas toast, and collard greens.

Terry had no appetite and he just sat there pushing his bloody steak around the plate like a little kid. His graving for H was like a living, breathing thing inside him. He needed to take a hit every other day or he felt crushed. After a while he excused himself and went down the dark hall to the opulent restroom. There was one guy at the urinals and Terry waited until he left. Then he checked the stalls to make sure they were empty and shut himself up in the last one on the right.

He took off his suit coat and hung it carefully on the back of the door. Then he removed the hypodermic syringe from its neat brown leather morocco case.

Rolling up his left shirtcuff, he plunged the needle into a sinewy vein and waited for the H to kick in. It always seemed to take a little more these days to get him where he needed to go.

And he never got there. It was never like the first time. Now he needed H just to get through the day, not to go crazy. It had become like oxygen, that essential.

Just when he thought it would never hit, his face suddenly burst into flames and his skin split along its seams. Violent coughs racked his throat until his eyes leaked water like a wound and the low lights of the restroom started spinning loops around him.

Ride it out, he thought. Ride it out until *it* passes.

When he returned to the table a few minutes later, he flagged down a waitress and ordered a couple more tall beers, but Lopez didn't want any and she told him she'd take an iced tea instead.

"Ah, c'mon," Terry urged her. "One more won't kill ya."

Now, suddenly, he sounded so impaired. It reminded her of one of those bad actors from the 70s playing a drunk, the kind that makes you think: that's not how it is, that's totally overblown. Noonan seemed to be speaking without moving his lips and there was barely a hitch in the pitch of his voice.

Lopez reluctantly took the beer and glared at him. His eyes were red and his skin was deathly pale, like a skeleton. Sweat soaked the collar of his bright yellow shirt. He looked like he might pass-out right there on the table.

He leaned back in his chair, and asked in a sliding, lugubrious slur, "So you think the Haywoods are already long gone, huh, boss?"

Lopez nodded her head. "Yeah, unfortunately I do. The roadblocks and air surveillance turned up nothing again. I think we were searching in the wrong spot. They're just north of here, I can feel it."

"So what do we do now?"

"We wait. I'm hoping Huddleston's roadblocks up in Sweetwater will turn up something. I really didn't want this," she said, setting the beer down on the table.

"Ah, it's all right," Terry said, sipping at his own tall glass.

"We have to be ready if something should happen," Lopez went on in a low voice, "and it takes clear heads."

"I ain't drunk," Terry said, between his teeth. "I'm just feeling good. There's nothing wrong with feeling good once in a while, is there, *Mary?*"

Lopez cleared her throat uncomfortably. It was the first time he'd called her by her first name and in some inconscient way, she didn't like it.

She watched him for a few seconds as he tipped the tall glass of beer into his mouth. His eyes were getting redder and redder, like they were going to catch fire.

When he finished his beer he reached over the table and asked if he could have some of hers. She told him he could have it and he drank it all in a few long gulps.

"You finished now?" Lopez said, her voice racked with scorn and recrimination. She was sick of his crap. He was nothing but a damaged soul, and she'd had way too many damaged souls in her lifetime.

Terry licked his lips and nodded thoughtfully. He stood up and his body felt very limp, as if it had been held together with stiff little wires and he stumbled at first. Lopez led him to the door and they went out. It was a warm night, the sky blanketed with stars and the gray moon hung in the east like a disfigured skull.

They crossed the street to the hotel. The guy at the front desk gave them a tired and familiar look when he saw the condition Terry was in. Lopez ignored him and led Noonan to the elevators. They got off on the third floor and walked the long corridor in silence until they reached Lopez's room.

Terry looked up at her and tried to give a smile, but it came out all wrong.

"Sorry about tonight," he said slowly, his tongue fumbling heavily over the words. "I guess I got a little fucked-up."

"Get some rest," she said. "I'll see you in the morning."

He nodded his head, and said, incomprehensibly: "Yes. You know, you're a great person to work with. A great lawman, I mean, woman. I mean—"

"Forget about it," Lopez said. "We'll talk in the morning, okay? Get some rest."

"Can I come in?"

"*What?*"

"Can I come in for a minute?"

Lopez's arms were rigid at her sides and her breath whispered. She said slowly:

"What the hell for?"

"I've seen—" Terry began, but he couldn't put the words together in the right order. It was like doing a crossword puzzle with only half the clues. His hand plowed through his long hair, over and over, tormentedly. "I've seen, Mary, the way you look at me—"

"Oh for God's sakes," Lopez said, lopping it off short. "Listen, Noonan, I don't know what you're on, but you better get your shit together. Let's just call it a night before one of us says something really stupid. Okay?"

"C'mon," he said, and she could smell the stench of alcohol on his breath and something more acidic leaking from his skin. He was pushing up closer to her now.

"Take it easy, Noonan," she warned in a sort of slow-rolling growl.

"We're both adults," he went on, too close to her now. "We both know what we want."

He had his hand on her arm and he was rubbing it up and down. He was almost pushing her up against the wall.

She kept her voice cold, dry: "C'mon, let's just stop this, okay?"

He leaned forward suddenly, put his left hand behind her head and kissed her on the mouth hard.

"Get off me!" she said, shoving him with both hands.

He stumbled back and almost lost his balance, but then he righted himself and was at her again. His right hand was trying to undo the top buttons of her blouse, while his left hand had moved down her leg and was trying to get under her little yellow skirt as his lips mashed against hers.

"You fucker!" she screamed, smacking him hard against the cheek and he stumbled back again.

He brought his hand quickly up to his face and started rubbing his red cheek.

"What the *fuck's* wrong with you?" Lopez said, her voice trembling.

"I'm sorry," he replied, so quietly she almost didn't hear him.

"You make me sick. I thought you were different, you know? But you ain't different. You're just like all the rest."

"I'm sorry. Mary—"

"Don't fucking call me Mary," she said with deadly quietness. "Just leave me alone."

She turned and opened the door to her room and slammed it on him without looking back.

Terry fell against the far wall. His head was spinning and his mouth was dry. Too dry.

How could he have been so stupid?

The funny thing about it was that Lopez was the first woman he had actually liked. All the women he had ever slept with in his sordid past and he never really liked any of them. It was sad. So Goddamn sad.

He tried to straighten up and stumbled down the long empty corridor toward his room. Even in his unstable condition, he wondered if she'd ever forgive him.

Chapter 23

The sky was a carpet of stars. It was too dark to see the landmarks. The little town of Red Cloud shone in the valley like a distant sublunary world, with its sea of lights spread out in an endless glittering sheet. The languid ray of a searchlight advertising an Indian casino across the river prodded about among the high faint clouds.

They went rolling into town on an empty tank of gas and Dick Haywood pulled the Silverado over at a Jenny on the outskirts of town.

"How much money you got?" he asked.

Robert took out his wallet and inspected its contents. He looked down and bit his lip but managed to maintain his composure.

"Not much. About twenty bucks."

"Okay," his father said. "I'll pay for the gas. I got a fifty. That's about all I got left. You run across the street there to that convenience store and get me some smokes, will ya, son?"

Robert nodded his head. "Anything else?"

"Nah, that's it. Meet me back here in ten minutes."

Robert got out of the truck and crossed the deserted highway to the small convenience store. It was one of those places that sold everything from milk to condoms to whiskey.

A little bell above the door jingled as Robert stepped in. There was a rack of magazines and local newspapers right inside the door and Robert picked up an *Abilene Star* and looked at it, half-expecting to see his picture on the front page with a wanted dead or alive heading above it. But there was nothing. Just a bunch of random meanderings about the national terror alert, an article about a man charged with internet fraud, another story about a mother and her three children who died in a mobile home fire up in Wichita Falls.

Robert set the paper back in its rack and walked up to the counter. All around the cash register, hanging down in colorful strips, were shiny lottery tickets printed up in bright colors—Hot Lotto, Mega Millions, Powerball, Pick 3, Cash 5—sucker bets, pitiful little prayers for some impossible dream.

"What can I get 'cha?" the kid working behind the counter asked. He was a short stocky black kid with squinted black eyes and a half smile.

"A pack of Marlboros," Robert said.

"Can I see some ID please?"

"What for?"

"The smokes."

"But I'm thirty-five years old," Robert said incredulously.

The kid shrugged his shoulders. "Boss says I gotta ID everybody under fifty. So I ID everybody under fifty. I ain't looking to lose my job, you know. They're hard to come by nowadays."

Robert shook his head and took his wallet out of the back pocket of his jeans. He took his driver's license out and handed it over the counter.

The kid held it up and looked at it. "Robert Haywood, huh? That's a nice name," he said, handing the ID back.

"Thanks," Robert said.

"I always wished my parents would have named me Frank Sinatra. Old Blue Eyes. I ain't got blue eyes, but—" the kid shrugged his shoulders again and let out a big laugh.

Robert liked this kid. He was a little off his nut, but a nice enough kid. He gave him the twenty for the cigarettes, took the change, and headed for the door.

"You have yourself a good night now," the kid called after him. "Stay out of trouble."

Robert smiled back. "You, too. Thanks, *Frank*."

He opened the door and the bell jingled again. He went out and crossed the highway. His father was sitting in the Silverado waiting for him.

"Did you get the smokes?" he asked.

Robert opened the passenger door and got in. He handed his father the cigarettes.

"What about the booze?"

"The what?" Robert asked.

"Where's the booze?"

"What booze?"

"I asked you to get me a bottle of Wild Turkey," his father said.

Robert shook his head. "No, you didn't."

"Yes. I did."

"No. You didn't."

"Jesus Christ," his father said. "I'll have to go get it myself then. Do I got to do *everything,* son?"

He opened the door and got out. Then he leaned his head back in, and said, "Swing the truck around and pick me up in a few minutes. Can you at least do that?"

Robert nodded his head and waved him off with the back of his hand.

"You never told me about no damn bottle," he said under his breath.

Dick Haywood crossed the highway, stood at the front of the convenience store for a moment, then went in.

The little bell above the door jingled and the black kid behind the counter nodded and his teeth flashed in a quick smile.

Black, sleepy-eyed son of a bitch, Dick Haywood thought to himself.

He went to the back of the store and picked out two bottles of Wild Turkey and brought them up to the counter.

The black kid smiled. "How we doing tonight, young man?"

"*Young man?*" Dick Haywood repeated with a smile. "I'm old enough to be your grandpa."

"Having a party tonight?" the kid asked, nodding toward the two bottles.

"Yep."

The kid grabbed the neck of the bottles and rang them up. "That'll be twenty-two fifty."

"No it won't," Dick Haywood said, his voice hollow, oddly distant.

"Whatcha talking about?" the kid said with a tight smile.

Dick Haywood stared at him perfectly straight-faced. "I believe these bottles will be on the house," he said, slowly reaching inside his coat and pulling out the old Army Colt .45. He said: "This is a gun, buddy. It goes boom-boom, and people fall down. Want to try it?"

The black kid's eyes were wide and startled. Dick Haywood moved the Colt up, so the muzzle was pointed directly at the kid's head.

With his other hand he motioned toward the cash register. "Clean it out, son."

The kid opened the register and took out some small bills and handed them across the counter.

"How about under the tray?" Dick Haywood winked. "That's where the big bills are, ain't they? Open it up and give 'em to me. Don't get smart neither, or I'll blow your black head clean off."

The kid lifted the tray and pulled out two one hundred dollar bills and handed them over.

"Now the safe," Dick Haywood said.

"What safe? There ain't no safe, mister."

Dick Haywood pointed the cold muzzle at the kid's face. "Stop fucking around. There's always a safe. How about over there, behind the smokes?"

The kid held his arms up in the air. Tears were streaming down his fat cheeks.

"Let me see the safe!" Dick Haywood screamed.

The kid moved the rack of cigarettes, revealing a small gray wall safe.

"See, what did I tell you," Dick Haywood said with a big smile. "There's always a safe. Now open it!"

"I can't."

"What?"

"It's timed. I can't open it."

"You ain't got the combination?"

"It's timed, mister. It ain't got no combination."

"You fucking with me, kid?"

The kid shook his head. "No I ain't, mister. I swear to you. I swear on my mother's grave."

Dick Haywood clicked the hammer back on the Colt. "Stop fucking around and open that damn safe or you'll be joining your poor mother."

The kid still had his hands up in the air.

"I can't—"

The Colt bucked and crashed out like thunder, making the room seem smaller and lowered-ceilinged than it was.

Then another shot rang out.

The kid's face convulsed.

He grabbed his belly with both hands and let out a strangled sort of yell/cry. He sagged slowly to his knees and fell on the floor face first. He lay there quite still, one half-open eyeball apparently looking up at Dick Haywood. He tried to open his mouth, but no sound came out of it.

Then he died on the floor.

Dick Haywood stood there and observed the kid for a couple of seconds. He was dead. Dead, but not quite cold yet, still only in the process of giving up the ghost.

Dick Haywood smiled and grabbed the bottles of booze and the money off the counter and walked away with no haste at all, toward the door with the little bell above it.

He walked out and tossed his cigarette away, watched it arc through the darkness and land in the gutter.

The Silverado pulled up beside him and he swung in beside Robert, and slammed the door.

"Get going fast," he said. "Stay off the interstate. Cops will be here in five minutes."

Robert looked over at him and said: "What did you do..."

His father held up the Colt, said swiftly and coldly: "Move, son!"

The gears kicked in, the Silverado jumped forward; Robert took a corner recklessly, the edge of his eye still on the gun in his father's unwavering hand.

"What happened to the kid in the store?" Robert asked. "I heard gunshots?"

His father said: "The kid stopped lead. He got cute. I had no choice. He's cold."

Robert found that his mind had gone blurred; everything was dissolving into a grayish, watery haze. He felt another weight drop on his shoulders and his stomach turned. He felt sick all over. He looked out the windshield at the dark breadth of pavement.

A car slid by now and then, two beams of white light attached to nothing, emerging from nowhere.

He spoke without taking his eyes off the road. "What did you do, Dad? He was just a *kid*."

"We needed the money. Tomorrow night we'll be back in Amarillo and it'll all be over."

Robert's entire body froze up and his head felt like it was going to explode. He kept thinking about Annie and the kids. *What would they do now when they found out this had happened?*

"It'll never be over," he finally said. "It'll never be over."

"Calm down, son," his father said. "Just calm down. Tomorrow we'll be in Amarillo. We'll be home. Then we'll collect that quarter million I hid. I'll split it with you fifty-fifty. Same as I said before. Stay calm. Just hang on, son. Don't blow it now when we're so damn close."

And then a rush of memories went through Robert's mind—memories of a life which was no longer his and had once provided him with the sweetest, simplest pleasures: warm sunshine and the smells of the ocean, the sky at dusk, Annie's smile and her laugh, the smooth pink skin and brown freckles on her back. The sweet loud laughter of his children. Things he had taken for granted just a short time ago.

The senselessness of what was happening seemed to take him by the throat. He felt like vomiting, and he had only one thought: to go home and get it all over with.

"It's over, Dad," he said, his face streaming with tears. "It all ends now. I'm ending it right now. I'm going to the police."

His father raised the Colt and held it steadily. "I can't let you do that, son. Don't be stupid. Think about your kids. Do you want them to grow up without a daddy? You go to the police and that's what'll happen. Are you ready to give up that cushy bank job of yours and retire to a penitentiary, for the sake of your morals? Or are you ready to grow up and be a man in a man's world, take your full responsibilities along with the rewards? You ain't the first guy in the world that ever got into a jam. Are you going to put up a fight, or are you going to fold up and go to jail? Because the police'll hang us *both* for killing those Mexicans back in the desert."

"It was self-defense. I'll tell them it was self-defense."

"It's too late for that now, son."

Robert looked over at him. "I fucking hate you. I hate your fucking guts," he said in a shattered voice, swinging the truck wildly, missing the ditch by inches.

Chapter 24

"When's Daddy coming home?"

Annie Haywood looked over at her son Jack and saw her husband in the boy. She missed Robert very much. She missed his smile, his laugh; his dark green eyes. It seemed like she missed him nearly every moment that she was awake. Once in a while she would forget and think about something else, then this heaviness would drop onto her shoulders and she'd start missing him all over again.

"Daddy will be back soon," she said, rubbing the thick blonde hair on top of Jack's head.

"I'm going to paint Daddy a picture," the boy said proudly.

"I'm going to paint him a picture, too," his sister Jenny said. She was at that stage where she copied everything her big brother did.

"That's great, you guys," Annie said, but her mind was somewhere else, her mind was on her husband.

After dinner she plopped the kids down in front of the television while she cleaned up and prepared baby Grace's bottle. Tonight was a special night. She was letting Jenny and Jack stay up late and have a popcorn party.

They watched Jack's favorite movie, *Star Wars: The Phantom Menace* on TBS. When the movie was finally over it was going on ten o'clock, so Annie turned the television off and rushed the kids upstairs.

She gave them all baths, put their p.j.'s on, read them books, said prayers, and by the time she got them tucked into their beds she was exhausted. Robert always told her that what she was doing—taking care of kids—was a full time job, and he was right.

It had been quite a late night, but she never seemed to be able to shut off the mental ticker tape that was her "*to do*" list.

They needed toilet paper, milk, toothpaste, and the faucet in the kids' bathroom had sprung a leak. Jenny had soccer practice tomorrow morning at nine, which started at the same time as Jack's football game over in Cliffside. Figure that one out. Baby Grace had come down with the *Ishies* and it could go either way in the night.

She was hoping Robert would call. She needed someone to talk to.

But when midnight came and he hadn't called yet, she figured he wasn't going to.

Oh, well, at least she was going to see him tomorrow night, she kept telling herself. He had been gone only a few days but it seemed like an eternity. She missed him badly.

Annie yawned and put the book down that she was reading. She got out of bed and took off her watch and earrings and bracelets and everything else. Then she went into the master bathroom and turned on the shower, nice and hot, just the way she liked it. The steam quickly filled the room and made her breathe easier.

She stepped under the spray and just let the water run through her. She washed her long blonde hair and let it fall down her shoulders. She thought of Robert again, how they used to take showers together before the kids came. They were a lot younger then. She wished he was in the shower with her now.

She rubbed the bar of soap over her arms and legs and waist. She still had a nice body for a mother of three. Robert still seemed to like it. Her stomach was relatively flat and well-muscled, except for a small bulge above her hips and around into her back. She could never get to that area. She did aerobics four times a week over at the Y, and she did a hundred sit-ups a day, but she still couldn't get at those little areas of flesh. *Love handles,* Robert teased her.

She rubbed the bar of soap across her breasts and felt the nipples. They were hard and big. She hated her nipples. They were too big. She wished she had bigger boobs and less nipple, but what the hell, you can't have everything. She thought of Robert's body. He had a perfect body. Perfect for her anyway. He wasn't skinny but he wasn't fat either. He was perfect. She liked a little meat on the bones. And his ass was in the same place as it was in college. Lucky bastard. She loved his ass. She thought of the *thing* between his legs and she could feel her nipples start to tingle. She never called his *thing* by its real name. She was too embarrassed. Sometimes she would call it Mister Peanut and sometimes John Henry after the guy with the big sledgehammer. But whatever she called it, she still loved it, even though it was ugly. All of them were ugly in a strangely erotic way. She thought of it now, him pulling it out of his jeans and her rubbing it before he put it in her.

After a while she turned off the water and got out of the shower and dried off with a huge crashy cotton towel. Back in the bedroom she slipped into her pajamas and lay down on the big bed.

She thought of Robert again and that long ride home ahead of him. God, she missed him. She couldn't wait until tomorrow night.

She reached over and turned off the light. Then she lay back down again and let her breath out at the ceiling.

Chapter 25

It was over now. His life was over. Everything he had worked so hard for was gone, washed away like a fallen tree during high tide.

Robert looked over at his father in the passenger seat. The old man sat there staring out the window at the cool dark night, his thin fingers gripping a cigarette, the gun resting in his lap.

He hated him. He hated everything about him. He wished he was dead.

Robert was driving slowly, trying not to draw attention to themselves. Police cars were speeding past them with their red lights flashing and their sirens howling towards the little convenience store on the edge of town.

"Why did you have to kill him?" Robert finally said, unable to hide the pain in his voice. "He was just a kid."

His father didn't answer. He brought the cigarette up to his mouth again and smoke speared from his nostrils in two malevolent columns. He looked like Satan.

"You didn't have to kill him."

"We need a new car," his father said, keeping his tone even, colorless.

His dark eyes were scanning the nearly deserted streets. He brought the cigarette up to his lips and blew smoke out the open window.

"There!" he said, pointing with his gun.

Robert focused his eyes to see what his father was pointing at.

There was a small parking lot behind a tavern on one corner of the street. It was very dark. Robert saw someone walking in the parking lot.

"Pull over," his father said.

"Why?"

"Just do it."

Robert flipped the blinker and turned right, into the parking lot. He moved the car slowly. On his father's side he could see a young girl walking quickly toward her car. She kept looking back at them over her shoulder.

His father smiled. It was the smile of a prisoner who has just found a file in a visitor's bakehouse pie.

"Pull up *right* next to her," he said.

"Why? What are you going to do?"

His father shrugged his shoulders and kept his tone even. "I'm going to ask this pretty young lady for a ride. That's all."

He smiled again and the tips of his gold teeth shone horrifically.

"No, Dad," Robert said. "I can't let you do that."

"Oh, yeah?" his father said. He held the Colt up steadily and threateningly. "And how you gonna stop me, son?"

"You got to be kidding?"

"I've never kidded about anything in my life," his father said. "I was born without a sense of humor. You should know that by now."

Robert slowed the car to a near stop beside the young girl. She was fumbling with her keys inside her purse. She looked to be about twenty years old, small and dark and delicately made. She was wearing a short black skirt, fuzzy sweater, and a lethal combination of white socks pulled up over the calves and shiny brown Mary Janes. A silver cross on a chain hung around her neck and fell between her rather small breasts.

Dick Haywood leaned his head out the car window. "Excuse me, ma'am?"

The girl looked up but kept her head low. She was chewing nervously on a piece of gum, her jaws snapping up and down like a turtle.

Dick Haywood flashed her a smile. "We were just wondering if you could tell us where Elm Street is at?" He used Elm Street because he knew every town—even in Texas—had an Elm Street. "We seemed to have gotten ourselves lost."

The girl spoke without turning her head towards him. "If you hang a left at the lights, and another left on Pineview, you should run into it."

Dick Haywood shifted the Colt between his chest and the door.

"A right at the lights, huh?"

The girl turned her head. "A *left—*"

But before she could finish Dick Haywood threw open the door and was out in front of her. He stuck the Colt in her ribs and told her to be quiet.

She made a small, miserable sound like a strangled sob, not quite a scream.

He said: "Let's not get any trickier than we have to...Maybe we'll have to—*enough.*"

The girl's face turned gray and she nodded her head very quickly.

"We're gonna go for a little ride," Dick Haywood said, pushing her hard up against her car. "Give me the keys."

She fumbled in her purse and handed him the keys. He opened the door and pushed her into the front seat, then he slid in behind the wheel and started it up and told Robert to get in.

Robert was still in the Silverado and he wasn't going to get out. He didn't care if his father shot him right there and then.

But now he had the girl to worry about. What would he do about the girl?

"Don't hurt me, mister," she was sobbing on the front seat. "Please don't hurt me."

"Shut up!" Dick Haywood screamed. Then he turned back to Robert. "Get in the fucking car, son."

Robert stared at him for a moment. Then he turned the Silverado's ignition off and stepped out of the truck.

He threw the keys into the night and walked slowly over to the girl's car, a little blue Volvo S60.

His father held the door open for him, then pushed him into the backseat.

"What are you going to do to me?" the girl cried.

"I told you, we're going for a little ride."

Dick Haywood put the car in reverse and backed up through the smashed glass of empty beer bottles in the tavern's parking lot and drove straight out onto the highway.

Straight north, Robert thought. Just north. Always going north and getting nowhere.

Chapter 26

"What's your name, sweetheart?" Dick Haywood asked the frightened girl.

She looked up at him. There were tears running down from the corner of her eyes. She rubbed the black mascara away with the back of her hand.

"I said what's your name, girl?"

"Helen," the girl said, her voice crackling like an old broken record.

"That's a nice name," Dick Haywood said. "Old-fashioned. What's your last name?"

"Garard."

"Well, Helen Garard, don't be afraid now. We just need you to help get us up to the state line. There, there, now, stop crying. It's all right, sugar."

Helen Garard sniffled and tried to catch her breath.

"What were you doing out so late by yourself, anyway?" Dick Haywood asked her.

"I just got off work," the girl said, trying to keep her voice from breaking. "I *waitress* at that bar back there. It helps pay my tuition."

"Oh yeah? Where do you go to school?"

"I'm a sophomore at Texas Christian."

Dick Haywood turned his head from the road and looked at her fuzzy sweater and black skirt and shiny brown Mary Janes. "That's what waitresses are wearing these days?"

She folded her hands across her lap and tried to subtly pull the hem of her skirt down over her thighs.

"How old are you?" he asked her.

"Nineteen."

Robert sighed. He was sitting in the back seat, wishing he was anywhere but here. He felt sorry for the girl. He couldn't even begin to imagine what she must be going through. Yeah, on second thought, he could. Because he was his father's hostage, too.

He wondered how he was going to get out of this without getting the girl killed. He no longer pretended to know what his father was capable of.

The girl looked back at him over the front seat. Her dark face was wet with tears and her eyes were twitching fearfully. She kept wiping at her face and putting her dark hair behind her ears.

Robert sat silently in back and watched the dark night pass by. They were back out on Highway 60, among the cornfields and grain silos, cutting across "The Divide," a stretch of land between the Salt Fork and the Champion Creek Brazos.

There were trees on both sides of the highway and Robert stared languorously up into them. He was half in and out of sleep, dreaming of Annie and of a place and time that seemed so long ago. He thought about being at Lake Meredith. Out there with Annie and the kids, with the sky above them, and the water around them, talking about how happy they were, and how it was going to last forever...

Chapter 27

After midnight they came to a roadblock just outside Justiceburg. Two State Trooper cars were parked face to face on the dark deserted highway. It was raining and beyond the flowing windshield the trooper lights wavered ruby-red in the darkness. The *click-click-click* of the Volvo's wipers was almost hypnotic.

It was very hot in the car. The windows were all shut and the glass was starting to fog up. The rain came down slantingly against the windshield and made a noise like drum-fire on the roof.

"All right," Dick Haywood said, peering out the windshield. "Everybody just be cool."

One of the troopers got out of his car when he saw the Volvo approaching. He was wearing a bright yellow rain jacket and a yellow hat with a slicker over it.

He held up his hands for them to stop.

There was a padded arm rest in the middle of the rear seat, and Robert leaned an elbow on it, cupped his chin in his hand, and stared through the half-misted windows. The rain was a thick white spray in the headlights. He wondered what his father was going to do now.

"Shit," Dick Haywood muttered under his breath. He pointed the revolver low at Helen Garard. "Play along smart and you won't get hurt."

The girl bit her bottom lip and nodded her head.

Dick Haywood put the gun back in his side coat pocket.

He brought the car to a stop and the yellow patrolman jogged over in the rain to the driver's side window.

Dick Haywood rolled down the window and smiled at the trooper.

"Hullo," the trooper said, rain dripping off the waterproof brim of his hat in little streamlets. "Wet enough for ya?"

"Joost about," Dick Haywood said, smiling. "What can I do for you, officer?"

The rain started coming down harder, thunder crackling in the distance. It was like the hills around them had been shaken up and were bumping around.

"What a night," the trooper said, wiping water off his face.

"Yeah, it is," Dick Haywood said, fingering the Colt in his pocket. "Is something wrong?"

The trooper narrowed his eyes. "Well, we got ourselves a little situation out here. We're looking for two men driving an old Chevy Silverado."

Robert was lying in the back seat and he was trying to keep his face from the trooper's view.

"What'd they do?" Dick Haywood asked.

"I'm not obliged to say," the trooper said.

Dick Haywood smiled. "Well, you can see this ain't an old Chevy Silverado." He nodded at Helen Garard on the seat next to him. "This is my daughter," he told the trooper.

"Who else you got *lying* in back there?" asked the trooper, nodding to the back seat.

Dick Haywood crooked his head. "Oh, that's my son-in-law. We were at a wedding down in Red Cloud; he had a little too much to drink."

The trooper brought a flashlight up and shined it in the back seat. Then he moved the flash around the inside of the car and up on the girl in the front seat. She looked a little young, but she sure was pretty. He shined the flash on Dick Haywood.

"You got a driver's license?" the trooper asked.

"Yes, I do," Dick Haywood said with a smile. "But the funny thing is; I forgot it back at home."

"You forgot it?" the trooper asked with a frown.

Dick Haywood sat up and started to pull the Colt out of his coat pocket. "Yep."

"Sir, I'm going to have to ask you to—"

"I have a driver's license," Helen Garard spoke up. "Will that help?"

The trooper looked at her for a moment. The rain was still dripping off his hat and into his face. He let out a sigh.

"That's okay, miss," he said, winking at her. Then he turned back to Dick Haywood and frowned. "Next time don't forget your driver's license. That's why you got it, you know."

"Yessir," Dick Haywood said, stuffing the Colt back into his pocket.

"Okay," the trooper said, "you folks have a nice night. And drive safely. It's raining dogs and polecats out here."

"Thank you, officer," Dick Haywood said with another smile. "We will. And you try to stay dry now, you here?"

"I'll try," the trooper said.

He waved a hand and the other patrol car blocking the road backed up, giving them room to pass.

Dick Haywood inched the Volvo forward in the dark rain and passed the trooper in the other car with a friendly wave and a smile, and the little blue Volvo slid through the rain without a whisper.

Chapter 28

He heard thunder. Deep, resonating booms that echoed through the small room. His blurry eyes opened slowly and he heard it again. The room was dark. He looked around.

It wasn't thunder.

Someone was knocking at the door.

Terry lifted his head and looked at the clock on the table next to the bed. The little red numbers were blinking: *2:32*.

"Who is it?" Terry called out, his voice stained by too much heroin, too many cigarettes, too much booze, and not enough sleep. Waking up wasn't like waking up anymore. When you got right down to it, he didn't think he had ever really been awake or asleep, at least in the way people used those words. It was almost like he was always asleep. Moving from one dream to another, his life an atelier of Chinese boxes or a hall of mirrors that never ended.

"Open up, Noonan! C'mon, open the door."

It was Lopez.

In a painful rush the memories of last night hit Terry square, as if he had just been belted in the face with a Louisville Slugger.

He tumbled out of bed and put on some pants. The breath was roaring in the back of his throat like he was some kind of an animal and his tongue was swollen in his mouth. His head was pounding.

"I'll be right there."

He hiccupped and looked at his face in the harsh white light thrown by the fluorescents over the mirror and tried to fix his disheveled hair but it was no use. Finally, he gave up and went to the door. When he opened it he saw Lopez standing there, her dark face done up and her beautiful black hair pulled back.

She put up her hand and said softly: "Hi."

"I'm sorry about last night," Terry said immediately. He stood quite still, smiling gently with his eyes, but not with his lips. The mango-sweet aroma of Lopez's perfume twitched at his nostrils.

"Let's just forget it ever happened," Lopez said, pushing her way into the room. "Just don't let it happen again."

Terry nodded his head soberly. "All right."

"How do you feel?" she asked.

"Like the inside of my head was a toilet," he said.

He looked at her more closely. She was wearing a smart black business suit that made her look tall.

"What's up?" he asked. "Do you always sleep like that?"

She smiled and walked through the room anxiously. Then the smile disappeared from her face and her voice became serious.

"There's been a murder up in a town called Red Cloud," she said, trying to control her emotions. "It's about twenty miles south of Clairemont. A kid working at a convenience store was shot to death, point-blank range. Video cameras mounted in the store caught it all on tape."

"Haywood?" Terry asked.

Lopez nodded, swiping a loose strand of hair over her ear. "Yep."

"Have the roadblocks in Sweetwater come up with anything yet."

"No."

"Maybe they're laying low for the night. Until the heat dies down. Did Haywood know he was being filmed?"

"I don't know," Lopez said. "I doubt it. The local authorities are holding the tape until we get there. It's about an hour drive from here."

"I'll take a quick shower and get dressed," Terry said. "Be out in a minute."

Lopez sat on the bed and waited. She heard the shower running and could see steam seeping out from the bottom of the closed door. A few minutes later the door opened and Terry came out. A towel was draped around his waist and his upper body was bare. His chest was as smooth as a teenage boy's, except for the kinky fringes around his nipples.

She looked at him as he hurried into the closet. He had a nice body, for someone so skinny. You couldn't tell by the loose suits he always wore, but he had a wealth of corded animal muscle on his skinny frame.

She had been thinking about him a lot lately. You know the way a person can get in your skull and stick there and you start to think about all his good traits and his bad ones too and then just about him as a person. That's the way she had been thinking about him lately. But his attitude last night made her a bit more apprehensive. She wondered what kind of drugs he was taking. He was a little off-kilter, but most of the time he seemed to have his shit at least half together.

A few minutes later Terry emerged from the bathroom wearing another olive suit and his expensive J.B. Hill cowboy boots.

"Ready," he said, giving Lopez a big smile.

They left the room and she paid the bill. Then they got in the Ford and Lopez turned it around onto Highway 60.

Buckets of rain fell out of the sky like tears and they sat in silence as they drove. The silence seemed to pour over them and smother them. It made them both feel awkward. Lopez finally broke it by reaching for the dashboard and snapping on the radio. A Country singer started singing about thunderstorms and neon signs. She moved the dial and a Rock-N-Roller screamed out sex and alcohol and speed. She moved the dial again and a rapper was going on about killing a cop and screwing a white woman.

"God, music sucks these days," she said.

She turned the dial again and came to an old station that was playing Mexican orchestras, a background of guitars strumming plaintively.

"Do you know what this is called?" she asked Terry.

He shook his head.

"*El Cuarto de Tula* by the Buena Vista Social Club. Always makes me kind of sad somehow. Makes me think of those boys that were killed in the desert."

"Why?"

"I don't know. I've been thinking about them a lot. I don't know whether I'm doing the Ruiz brothers right or not."

"Well, quit worrying about the Ruiz brothers," Terry said. "If it hadn't been Dick Haywood that killed them, someone else would have eventually."

"I was just thinking about them." She paused for a long time and kept her attention on the road. When she spoke her voice was low. "Have you ever had to kill someone in the line of duty, Noonan?"

He peered at her hard. "Yeah. Once. How about you?"

"No. Not yet." She paused again, then asked, "How did it happen?"

"You mean when I had to kill someone?"

She nodded her head.

"It was fucked up." He lit a cigarette, drew deeply, casually exhaled. "It never should have happened. She had a gun."

"It was a *woman?*"

"Yep," he said, a distant quality in his voice. "I was working on this case, helping out on a murder investigation up in Farnsworth. Turns out the sheriff that I was helping—a woman—was the killer. When I threw down on her she pointed a shotgun at my face. I had no other choice. You learn to live with it. You tell yourself it was fate, that's all. We have to expect it in our line of work."

"I'm still waiting for the day when I have to—" She couldn't even say it. "I dread it every day I put on my gun. I keep praying that it never happens."

Chapter 29

They were almost to Lubbock now. They had skirted around the city of Grassland and blew by Pleasant Valley without stopping. They met hardly any traffic and at the town of Woodrow, Dick Haywood stopped the car. It had quit raining and the night was thick and murky. No moon, no stars, the sky just a bucket of black paint someone had accidentally kicked over.

"What are you doing?" Robert asked from the backseat.

"We need a place to rest for a few hours."

The girl in the front seat was almost sleeping. Dick Haywood shook her awake.

"Wake up, sugar," he said, his voice rough and road-weary.

Helen Garard opened her eyes. She looked around the car for a minute. It was like she didn't remember where she was and what had happened.

Dick Haywood pulled the car into a little motel on the side of the highway called the Broke Spoke.

"Are you going to let me go now?" the girl asked in a low voice.

"We'll let you go, honey," Dick Haywood said. "But not now. When we get where we need to be, that's when we'll let you go. Now we have to rest for a few hours."

"No stopping," Robert said from the backseat.

"What?" his father said, in a very tired, distant voice.

"No stopping," Robert said. "I want to get *home* as soon as possible."

Dick Haywood gave him a scowl through the rear view mirror. "We've been driving for two days straight. We need rest, son."

"I want to get home."

"Stop your whining." He held up the gun just so Robert and the girl remembered it was there. "Now go and get us a room." He nodded his head at the girl so Robert would know he wasn't fooling around. "And no funny stuff, understand, son?"

Robert got out of the car. Then he leaned back in against the driver's side window.

"How am I supposed to pay for the room? I have no money left."

His father reached into his jeans pocket. He took out a wad of bills he had stolen from the convenience store and shoved them in Robert's fist.

Robert turned around. As he walked across the gravel parking lot he looked up at the moon peeking out from behind the gray clouds, and he could picture the man up there laughing down at him.

Robert opened the glass front doors of the motel and walked in.

The fat guy sitting behind the front desk tried unsuccessfully to hide the Penthouse magazine he was reading.

"What can I do ya?" the fat man asked.

"I need a room," Robert said.

"Kinda late, ain't it?"

"What's it to you?" Robert said, keeping his head low.

The fat man held up his hands. "Hey, it's nothing to me." He took out an old-fashioned registry from behind the desk. "How many beds you want? One or two?"

"Two."

"Okey-dokey. If you'll just sign here..." He pushed the registry toward Robert.

Robert signed it: Ben Shockley. It was the first phony name that popped into his head. A character Clint Eastwood once played or something.

"Okey-doke," the fat man said again. "That'll be fifty-nine dollars and ninety-nine cents. We accept checks, credit, or..."

Robert slapped a wad of crumpled bills on the desk. The fat man counted out the money and handed him a key to Room 21.

"It's around the corner and up the stairs," the fat man said. "Try to be as quiet as you can. We run a respectful business here."

Robert gave him a distant look. "I'll bet you do."

He took the key and walked out, looking over his shoulder once and saw that the fat man had returned to his Penthouse.

Back at the car his father got out and handed Robert their bags. Then he picked up the bottles of whiskey he stole from the convenience store and grabbed the girl out of the front seat. He stuck the Colt in her ribs and told her to move.

They went around the building and up the stairs to Room 21.

Robert opened the door and went in. His father pushed Helen Garard inside, looked around, and then shut the door.

It was a small room that smelled of must and sin, with two small beds and a reading lamp on the desk that shed glow on the shabby carpet and the long heavy red drapes across the windows. Its light fell on the armchair in which Robert sat.

Dick Haywood told the girl to sit down on one of the beds. He took off the black leather belt with the silver buckle he was wearing around his jeans.

"I'm sorry I've got to do this, sugar" he told her. Then he tied her wrists above her head to the bedpost with the leather belt.

He grabbed her ankles and gently placed her legs on the bed. The short black skirt she was wearing rose above her thighs and showed her good young legs.

Robert sat in the chair and watched his father closely.

"Okay, all right," his father suddenly said, pacing back and forth across the small room. "We just got to get us some rest. Then everything we'll be all right; everything will be jake."

He sat down on the other bed and took out one of the bottles of whiskey and peeled off the cap. His hands were shaking as he brought the bottle to his dry lips. He held it out to Robert.

"No," Robert said.

His father turned the bottle up again. Then he held the bottle out to the girl on the bed. She shook her head. Her face was as white and hard as scraped bone.

"I'm just so goddamn tired," Dick Haywood said, running a wrinkled brown hand across his face. "I'm not as young as I used to be."

The girl sat listening to him, periodically glancing over at Robert with a nervous look on her face. She kept moving her hands in the belt, as if trying to get circulation in them.

"Is the belt too tight?" Dick Haywood asked, standing up off the bed.

The girl shook her head and he sat back down. The dreggy contents of the whiskey bottle jostled as he shook it around. He drank.

"You sure you don't want some?" he said, holding it out to Robert.

Robert said nothing.

His father took another sip and stared off at the dark walls.

"I made some mistakes when I was young," he said, almost to himself. "But when you're young you don't see things. Those things haunt me every day. I should have been a lawyer or at least a banker like you, son. I should have robbed people with my brain instead of my gun. But I never was cut out for that type of life, sitting behind a desk for eight hours a day, kissing people's backsides. I guess I should have changed my name to Hannibal, or maybe just Rex."

He drank again.

"I know we're in this a lot deeper than I planned to be, son."

"The bottom's fell out now, Dad," Robert said. "You shouldn't have killed that boy. The others were self-defense. But we're gonna fry now for sure." He shook his head and he could see the girl staring frightfully at him from across the room. "The bottom's fell out. There's no way up to the top anymore. Even the light at the top is black."

"You could find a lawyer," Helen Garard said.

Both Robert and his father stared at her. It was the first full sentence she had uttered.

Dick Haywood said: "The way I figure is this, when the law gets me again I won't be in any shape for a lawyer."

He took a long pull off the bottle. Spilled liquor wet the lines in his chin, ran over his Adam's apple and down his neck. His words were slurred now.

"I'm not sorry for anything I ever did in this world. I'm just a black sheep and there's no getting around it." He paused and stared at Robert for one drunken moment. "But I love *you,* son. You've done all right by me. Sometimes when a flower goes bad another rose will bloom..."

Distant, tiny, taut wires shrilled in Robert's ears. The girl, Helen Garard, was peering at him hard. Robert stared back at her.

"I don't like to look behind," his father went on in a drowsy voice. "I try just to think of the good things. But I guess I know what's going to happen eventually." He laughed cheerlessly, and then a chill like the morning air came into his voice. "Don't you feel it, son?"

Robert pierced his brows and glared at his father.

"Don't you feel it?" his father said again. "Don't you feel it in your stomach? That feeling? That burning sensation in your gut that means you're alive? Of not knowing what's going to happen next? What's in store for you around the next bend? That's called *life,* son. You just don't get that settin' behind a desk all day. Gawd, I love that feeling. I live for that feeling."

"I don't feel it, Dad. I don't feel it, okay? I don't feel anything at all. Except fear. It's like dying when you're still alive. Like being buried and you wake up and you're not dead. I just want to go home. I just want to be with my wife and kids."

His father was staring off now, one hand precariously gripping the bottle of booze. It looked like it was going to fall and bust up all over the floor.

His eyelids hung heavy and the gray pupils were shot with tiny red streaks. The girl on the bed kept looking at him and then back at Robert. Her legs on the bed were clean and smooth and very young. Her long black hair fell over her shoulders in waves. She was really quite beautiful. Face like a puckering kiss and ears with the tiniest lobes. Pierced lobes, but no earrings. Just the hurtful little mark. Her eyes like gold dust, the eyebrows soft, unshaped, just brushed faintly with black to darken them. The short black skirt was pulled high above the slope of her pink thighs. Her polished leather shoes and white socks sticking to her ankles, so tight around her calves.

Dick Haywood finally put the nearly empty bottle on the floor beside the bed and fell upon the pillows with a muffled grunt. The girl kept looking at him, then back at Robert.

When she was sure the old man had fallen asleep, she whispered to Robert: "He's going to kill me. You know that, don't you?"

"What?"

She nodded her head at Dick Haywood, passed out on the other bed. "Your father. He's going to kill me. He can't let me go. He won't let me go."

Robert shook his head. "He's not going to kill you." He paused and looked at the girl and her dark eyes. "I won't let him kill you."

"I see it in his eyes. It's the same look I see from the dirty old men...who sit in their cars and watch me walk to school."

"I won't let him touch you," Robert said.

"You promise?"

He nodded his head and whispered: "*I promise.*"

He had never broken a promise, never, and he never intended to.

She smiled. It was the first time he had seen her smile. It was such a pretty smile. It reminded him of his daughter Jenny's smile.

The ringing in his ears was almost deafening. Outside it was raining again, harder now, the wind whistling in the window-screen and water slashing in the puddles under the eaves.

Robert got up and pulled a blanket off his father's bed and gently draped it over Helen Garard. Then he sat in the chair, watching the girl's form, listening to her breathing. Her arms were over her head and tied to the bedpost. She was tired and scared. Her eyes kept scanning the room and looking out the window.

She sucked in a deep breath through her mouth and nose. She jerked convulsively, and tried to keep herself from dropping off to sleep. She jerked again, easier though, and now her mouth was closed and she was asleep.

The ringing in Robert's ears finally faded far, far away and his eyes grew heavy and he closed them...

He kept dreaming about jail and the electric chair. About being locked away; locked up in a cell. He kept waking up in a sweat with the sound of the heavy rain in his ears and sitting in the shadows smoking a cigarette and dropping off to sleep again and waking up out of another nightmare.

Chapter 30

With its two blocks of gas stations and restaurants on the north side of the widened highway and then the intersecting, one-block Main Street, the town of Red Cloud, Texas had a business district shaped like a cone. The cone's entry was foggy with low buildings of brick and wooden frames.

With Lopez driving, they moved up Main Street toward the convenience store at the end of the block. It was three-thirty in the morning. The thunder had passed and the lonely moon hung in the gray sky like a shred of fingernail.

Lopez parked the car behind a gaggle of police vehicles and ambulances, their lights reflecting upon the wet street.

They got out of the car and entered the store. The little bell above the door jingled as they stepped in.

Inside there was such silence and so much dead air it did not seem the store could have been entered for days. There was one uniformed police officer standing by the door and a plain-clothes cop hovering around the cash register.

When Lopez and Terry entered, the plain-clothes cop behind the register turned around.

"Are you the Feds?" he asked.

Lopez nodded her head.

"I'm Detective Danders," he said in a pleasant but weary voice. "I'm with the Red Cloud Police Department. I've been keeping everybody out of here until you guys arrived."

Danders was a tall man, with a long bony face and hair the color of wet sand. He had thin smoker's lips and a thin straight nose that divided his face like an immaculate stone wall. His eyes were ice cold blue and he had small wrinkles around the edges. He held a Styrofoam cup of blazing hot coffee in one hand, a cigarette in the other, the smoke from both swirling up into his eyes.

Lopez motioned with her head toward the register.

"What have you got?" she said.

Danders looked back over his shoulder with a grimace. "We got a dead kid," he said. "Just twenty years old. Care to have a look?"

Danders walked behind the register and held out his hands. His movements were slow, thoughtful, almost absent-minded.

Lopez and Terry followed him behind the register.

The black kid was lying in a puddle of greasy-looking blood. His face was gray with death and fright. There were two gaping holes in his chest and abdomen. His wide dead eyes were bulging out of his face. They had the effect the eyes of the new dead have, of almost, but not quite, looking at you.

Lopez moved slowly across the floor, around the body without touching anything. She looked down at him, shook her head. He was just a kid. A kid just doing his job, working his way through college or something.

She kneeled down on one knee, cocked her head on one side, and touched him.

"Two shots," she muttered. "Look like .45's—hard slugs. Close to the heart. At least he died pretty quickly. A minute or two tops."

Danders made a disgusted sound and walked to the window, stood with his back to the corpse, looking out at the wet dark streets.

Lopez held one of her hands to the dead kid's skin and lifted a dead eyelid. "Has the print or camera men been here yet?" she asked.

"No," Danders said. "No one has been in here yet except me and him." He nodded his head toward the uniformed cop guarding the door.

Lopez looked back at the corpse and then up at Danders.

"Dick Haywood did this?" she asked.

"Yep," Danders said. "There's a camera mounted on the wall there. It got everything."

"Can we see those tapes, Detective?"

"Sure," Danders said. "They're in the back office. Follow me."

He turned to the uniform standing at the door, and said, "Nobody gets in. I don't care who it is, don't let them in."

Danders led Lopez and Terry to a windowless room in the back of the store. It was dark and damp and smelled of cardboard. There was a television and VCR in one corner of the room and Danders turned it on.

The screen flickered to life:

The black kid is standing behind the cash register. Dick Haywood appears on screen, and stands in front of the kid. He puts two bottles down on the counter and then he exchanges words with the kid which are not picked up on the tape.

Dick Haywood smiles.

The kid grabs the neck of the bottles and rings them up. More words are exchanged.

Then Dick Haywood stares perfectly straight-faced into the camera. And winks.

He reaches inside his coat and pulls out the old Army Colt .45.

He points it at the kid's face.

Terry took his eyes off the television screen for a brief moment. He looked over at Lopez but she didn't return his gaze. She was too focused on what was happening on screen...

With his other hand Dick Haywood motions toward the cash register.
The kid opens the register and takes out some bills and hands them across the counter.
Dick Haywood says something and the kid lifts the tray under the register and pulls out two one hundred dollar bills and hands them over.
Dick Haywood points the cold muzzle at the kid's face again. It looks like he says something. Perhaps: "Stop fucking around" and something about a safe.
The kid holds his arms up in the air. Tears are streaming down his cheeks.
Dick Haywood screams.
The kid turns and shoots a quick glance up at the camera. Then he moves the rack of cigarettes and exposes the safe in the wall.
Dick Haywood smiles and says something to the kid.
The kid shakes his head.

"The kid can't open the safe," Danders put in. "It's timed. No combination."

Dick Haywood is screaming now.
The kid shakes his head again.
Dick Haywood clicks the hammer back on the Colt.
The kid still has his hands up in the air. His lips mouth the words:
"I can't—"
Dick Haywood pulls the trigger.
And again.

Lopez let out a little muffled cry and covered her mouth with her hand.

†††

The kid's face convulses. He grabs his belly with both hands and lets out a strangled sort of cry that is silent on the screen. Then he sags slowly to his knees and falls on the floor face first. He lays there quite still, one half-open eyeball apparently looking up at Dick Haywood. He tries to open his mouth, but nothing comes out of it.

Then he dies on the floor.

Dick Haywood stands above him for a couple of seconds. He grabs the bottles off the counter and walks away without haste, toward the door with the little bell above it.

The tape ended and Lopez breathed out slowly, stood up, and then turned away.

"We'll need a copy of that tape," she said to Danders.

"Certainly." He paused a moment, looked her in the eye, and said, "You're gonna catch this bastard, right?"

She turned her head slowly and looked at Danders. Her voice faltered a little, saying:

"Yes, Detective. We're gonna catch him."

She thanked him for his assistance and went quickly out of the tiny office. Terry followed her through the store and out the door onto the street. It was starting to get warm and it smelled wet, like things after a rain storm.

"I should have done something to prevent this," Lopez said, pacing back and forth in front of their car.

"What could you have done?" Terry asked.

"I don't know. Maybe I should have made contact with Haywood sooner. Maybe that kid would still be alive if I had..."

Terry took out a cigarette and rolled it between his fingers. He lit it slowly and waved the match until it went out. "You could have never seen it coming."

Lopez stared at him without expression. She said slowly:

"I should have listened to you." Her voice was as dead as the kid back in the store. "You told me we should make contact with Haywood."

Terry drew on the cigarette he held cupped in his hand.

He said in a tone that meant nothing: "So what do we do now? You ready to call him now?"

She looked up at him, then ahead again. "Why me?"

Terry shrugged. "You're running the show. You're in charge."

"But you know Dick Haywood. You've arrested him before."

"What does that matter?"

"He'll listen to you."

"Maybe. Maybe not." Terry paused, rubbed the end of one eyebrow, and went on: "Okay, I'll make the call. But things have changed. I say we make contact with the kid instead."

"Robert Haywood?" Lopez asked. "Why him?"

"Because I have a feeling he wants out. I would if I was in his situation—"

The door to the convenience store suddenly opened and Detective Danders was sprinting toward them with an urgent look painted on his skinny face.

"I just got a call," Danders said, breathing a smoker's heavy breath. "It appears a man matching Dick Haywood's description was seen a couple of hours ago in the parking lot of a local bar. A witness says he saw two men in the parking lot abducting a girl who worked at the bar."

"Where was this?" Lopez asked.

"Just on the edge of town."

"Who's the girl?"

"Name's Helen Garard. Local girl."

Terry said: "Has her parents been notified? What about the local media?"

Danders shook his head. "No media. Not yet. But the girl's parents know. Her Dad is a big wig in the local political scene. A judge or something. One of our local cops tipped him off. Mother's a lawyer. They got more money than God."

"Can we meet them?" Lopez asked. "Maybe they can give us some information about their daughter, provide a picture or something."

"I'll see what I can do," Danders said. "I'll make a few phone calls; see if I can get you a face to face with the parents. They got a big house up on top of the hill, overlooking the Salt Fork Brazo."

Chapter 31

The big brick house on top of the hill stood a long way back from the narrow, winding ribbon of concrete that was called Summit Avenue. It wasn't a house, *mansion* was definitely a better word for it; a three-story Spanish-style edifice. It had to have run at least fifteen-thousand square feet, maybe even more, rising out of the dawn behind a sweep of lawn as big as a golf course and trimmed as close as a French poodle.

There was an arch above the front entrance and ivy on the wall. Large magnolias grew all around the facade, very close to it, and made it a little dark and remote.

Lopez was following Danders' late-model tan-colored unmarked around the oval driveway and parked behind him in front of the ivy arch. They all got out of their cars simultaneously and walked slowly up the path of stepping stones. Their heels clicked on the stones like soldiers in march.

The sky was still dark, but there was a hint of sun peeking over the horizon, like blood from an open wound.

Danders reached out and pushed a bell at the side of the door, almost hidden by the creeping ivy.

There was a long wait. It was very cool, very silent. Terry looked up at the ivy gables.

"Nice place," he said with a whistle.

"Not too shabby," Danders agreed.

The door opened slowly and a woman's face peered out, a long, sad face with tear streaks on its ashen cheeks. The face almost smiled, said haltingly:

"Yes, can I help you?"

Danders took out his wallet and showed her his identification.

"Miss Garard, I'm Detective Danders. I spoke to you earlier on the phone."

"Oh, yes, yes. Please come right in."

Susan Garard stood aside and let them into a shadowy hall with a marble floor. She was about fifty years old, thin, with light gray hair and a smooth, lean face. Her warm brown eyes were stunned; doped with shock.

"My husband is in the library," she said.

They followed her along the marbled hall to the back of the house, turned into another hall.

Susan Garard knocked at a door, turned the knob and led them into a big room that was dim in spite of its many windows. Big magnolia trees grew close to the windows, pressing their leaves against the glass.

The tall man in the middle of the room didn't look at them when they entered. He stood motionless, stiff. He was staring out the windows. His hands were tightly clenched behind his back.

After a while Danders spoke through the silence, in a low, husky voice.

"Mister Garard, I'm Detective Danders, with the Red Cloud Police Department." He paused and nodded toward Terry and Lopez. "This is Special Agent Noonan with the Texas Rangers and Agent Lopez with the FBI."

Jonathan Garard turned his head slowly and looked at them. He was a handsome man, tall, heavy-set and athletic, but the skin on his face looked dim, like the bottom of a pool of water. Lights shifted in his hair. A touch of gray glinted in it. His eyes were vividly, startlingly blue.

He was wearing a dark suit, white shirt, black tie. What he wears at funerals, Lopez thought.

"Tell me, Agent Lopez," Jonathan Garard said in a dead voice, with no formalities. "Why has the FBI become involved so quickly in this matter?"

Lopez cleared her throat. "We have reason to believe that a suspect we have been trailing may be involved in your daughter's abduction."

"This suspect, who is he?"

"His name's Dick Haywood."

"What did he do?"

Lopez cleared her throat again. "He was involved in a dispute with several men down in Mexico."

"A *dispute?*" Jonathan Garard said, his thick brows raised. "Did he kill these men?"

Lopez nodded her head, and said, "Yes. Yes, we believe he did."

A little muffled cry escaped from Susan Garard's tight lips. She sank into a large leather sofa by the fire and swiped her eyes with a starched handkerchief. Then she looked up at Lopez, and asked:

"Has this man been in trouble before?"

Now Terry put in: "Dick Haywood's been arrested several times for minor misdemeanors and robbery in the past."

Susan Garard said slowly: "Has he even been arrested for se—" Her voice broke and she could not go on.

Her husband finished it for her: "Has he ever been arrested for any kind of...sexual assault?"

"No."

A show of relief spread momentarily across Jonathan Garard's face. He asked: "Is this man alone?"

"We believe his son is traveling with him," Lopez said. "The son may just be an unwilling accomplice."

"Well, there's your lead—" Jonathan Garard said with whispered vehemence, the voice of a judge who's seen plenty of crimes, but has never investigated one. "You should make contact with this son. Work on him and break him. Make him end this now."

Lopez glanced across the room at Terry for a moment. Then she looked back at Garard, and said, "Yes, we have every intention of doing just that, sir."

There was a long silence and the room felt hot and stagnant. Jonathan Garard moved across the room and stood behind his crying wife on the sofa, rubbing her slender shoulders.

Lopez waited a moment before speaking. "Mister Garard, we understand your daughter had just gotten off work at the Lamplighter Saloon before she was...abducted."

"Yes, that's right."

"Was she a waitress?"

"No." Jonathan Garard paused and glanced at Danders and at Terry for a moment.

"Did she tend bar?" Lopez asked.

"No." He paused again, then reluctantly and with a touch of discomfiture, he said, "She's a dancer."

"A dancer?"

"A stripper, Agent Lopez," Garard said bitterly. "My daughter is a stripper."

Lopez briefly looked around at the rich opulence of the room. "I don't understand, sir. I thought Helen was a student at Texas Christian University."

"She was, I mean she *is*," Jonathan Garard said in a husky tone. "She didn't need the money, if that's what you're getting at. She did it to spite me. Can you understand that, Agent Lopez?"

Lopez remained silent.

"No, I didn't think you would," Jonathan Garard said piercingly. "Do you have children, Agent Lopez?"

Lopez shook her head.

Jonathan Garard continued dryly. "Then you'll never understand. But I still love her. Can you *understand* that, Agent Lopez?"

Lopez nodded somberly for a moment. Then she said, "Mister and Mrs. Garard, I assure you, we will do everything in our power to return your daughter to you unharmed."

Susan Garard looked up from the sofa and stared directly into Lopez's dark eyes.

"I believe you," she whispered.

Jonathan Garard walked out from behind the sofa and returned to the windows and stood staring out.

After a moment, in a voice almost too soft to be heard, he said, "I want you to *kill* him."

"I beg your pardon, sir?" Lopez said.

"I want you to find this Dick Haywood, and I want you to kill him."

"Sir—?"

"Just find him and kill him!" he screamed. "I know you can do it. I'll pay you if that's what it takes. I want my baby back. Just find him. Find him and kill him. Just fucking kill him!"

Chapter 32

Robert was dreaming of Annie when his cell phone rang. It was turned down low and barely audible, but he could feel it vibrating against the inside of his leg.

He opened his eyes quickly and focused them against the dimness of the motel room. His father was still passed out on the far bed and the girl, Helen Garard, was sleeping on the other, her lips slightly parted, her head leaned back against the bed. The blanket he had draped over her earlier in the night had been kicked off and lay on the floor. She looked like a sleeping princess waiting for the kiss of a deliverer. How helpless she looked in sleep. Her hands were still tied to the bedpost above her head and the little black skirt she was wearing had shifted up her legs even further. Robert could see all of her good thighs now and a hint of pink panties between her legs.

The cell phone buzzed again, lightly, vibrating in his pants pocket.

He got up quickly from the chair and went into the bathroom, shutting the door softly behind him.

He clicked the talk button, and whispered, "Hello?"

"*Robert Haywood?*"

It was a man's voice, hard and serious. The voice was not familiar to him.

Robert let the line go silent for five, ten, fifteen seconds.

"You still there, Robert?"

"Yeah, I'm here," Robert said. "Who's this?"

"My name is Terry Noonan. I'm an officer with the Texas Rangers."

Robert felt as though his feet were slipping on ice, like the world had suddenly tilted and he was falling off it into the dark, and would fall and fall forever because there was no end to the place where he was falling.

"What do you want?" he said, gripping the phone very tight.

"We know what happened...out there in the desert. We know it wasn't your fault, Robert. There was nothing else you could do...right?"

"Yes," Robert whispered, "that's right."

"Yes, and we know what happened to that boy at the convenience store. It was all on tape. We saw your father shoot that boy."

"I didn't want that to happened," Robert said. "I didn't want any of it to happen."

"We know, Robert, we know. But now there's a girl involved, isn't there? Robert, listen to me, is there a girl there with you? Is Helen there with you now?"

"Yes," Robert said. "I don't know why he took her. I don't know why any of it happened."

"We know, Robert. We're here to help you. You want to go home, don't you? You want to see that pretty little wife of yours and those three great kids, right?"

"Yes. That's all I want right now..."

"I can help you. But you got to let me help you, Robert. Robert, are you listening?"

"Yeah, yeah, I'm listening."

"We know you didn't have anything to do with the murders. We know it was your father that did it."

But it wasn't, Robert thought to himself. I killed those Mexicans. I killed them. It wasn't my fault. I didn't mean to kill them. I killed them.

"*Robert, you still there?*"

"Yeah."

"*The girl can't be hurt. It's up to you, Robert. You need to help us bring her back to her parents. You've got two girls of your own, don't you, Robert?*"

"Yes."

"*How would you feel if someone stole one of your daughters away from you? What would you do? Do it now, Robert. Help me, Robert.*"

"How?"

"*There's a little town called Wayside, just before you get to the city line of Amarillo. Not much of a town really. Robert, you listening?*"

"Yeah."

"*There's a filling station on the edge of Wayside, on Highway 60. One of those old Sinclair filling stations. The ones with the dinosaurs. Across the highway from the filling station there's a restaurant. It's nothing but a roadside barbeque joint, like a million others you see on the highway. I want you to go there, Robert. Park in the filling station and get some gas. Then make an excuse why you and Helen have to go to the restaurant across the highway. I don't care what you do; just get the girl into the restaurant. Do you understand what I'm telling you?*"

"Yeah, I understand."

"*Good.*"

"Then what happens?" Robert said. "What happens to me and my dad?"

"*We wipe the slate clean, Robert. If you help us, we'll grant you immunity.*"

"And my father?"

"*He'll be all right. We'll arrest him. He'll do some time. I'm not going to bullshit you. He'll do a lot of time. But we won't hurt him. If he pleads, he may not get the death chair. This is your chance, Robert. It's your only chance to see your family again.*"

Robert knew what it meant. He would have to trade his soul. He'd have to give them his father to save his self. He'd have to sacrifice his father like a goddamn Judas.

"Do we have a deal, Robert?"

Robert nodded his head, hard lines at the corners of his mouth. He slid down the wall of the claustrophobic bathroom and sat on the floor, holding the phone tight to his ear.

The words had a hard time coming out, he was so tired. "Yeah," he said. "We've got a deal."

"Okay then, Robert. I'll see you soon..."

Robert hung up so slowly that the loss of line was barely audible. His hand stayed on the phone, then fell away to his side.

He sat on the floor and...

...the door to the bathroom suddenly came crashing in on him and his father stood there like a raving thing.

His white hair was sticking up all over the place and the stubble on his face looked silvery, like fungus growing on a corpse.

He moved like an explosion. He snatched the phone out of Robert's hand, smashed it to pieces on the floor, and kicked it into a corner, his breath coming quick and rapid.

"Who were you talking to?" his father shouted, tiny streams of spittle flying out of his blue lips.

Robert looked up at him, and for a moment he didn't recognize this thing standing above him. In his eyes was the strained seething look that always frightened him. At such times his father's eyes did not look straight ahead but vacillated and seemed to be looking at nothing. It was like an invisible curtain had come between the man and all the rest of the world, like a little volcano that lies dormant for years and then suddenly spouts fire.

"Who the fuck were you talking to?" his father shouted again. "Answer me, boy, or I'll beat your ears down."

Robert stammered. "No...no...Nobody. I wasn't talking to anyone."

"I heard you. I heard you talking."

"I called Annie. She didn't answer so I left a message."

"How long were you on that goddamn thing?"

"Just a few seconds," Robert said. His voice was shaking.

"Don't you know they can track you on those things?" his father said. "I already told you that. They got satellites up in the sky that track 'em. Jesus Christ, son, you got to smarten up."

Dick Haywood shook his head and turned toward the door. Then he gave one last stomp at the ruined cell phone and went out of the room.

Robert stood up quickly and shut the door. In the small bathroom he felt confined, trapped, and yet, safe. Waves of nausea sent him to the toilet, where he knelt in front of it on all fours, until a vile liquid bubbled up from the pit of his stomach.

It tasted like blood and burned the back of his throat. His head was spinning and he thought he might pass out.

He needed to clear his head. He felt dirty and miserable, so he slid back the crunchy plastic shower curtain and turned on the hot water.

He stripped off the clothes he had been wearing for the last two days and ducked under the spray. He stood under it and soaped himself, rubbed his whole body over, kneaded his muscles, rinsed off. It felt good, the water pelting his back and flowing through his hair. He missed Annie and the kids and he wanted to be home. The shower always reminded him of home. It was where he went to clear his head, the last great sanctuary in the midst of three loud kids, a huge mortgage nearing bankruptcy, a shaky job, two car payments, and a grocery bill that exceeded $500 a month. But those things were trivialities compared to the mess he was in now.

He took out a disposable razor and brought it to his rough cheeks and chin. The stubble was getting thick, and several times he nicked his skin and he watched—as if in a dream—the blood as it flowed down the drain.

He felt as if he was falling apart.

Something beyond the closed door knocked hollowly and the razor slipped out of his hand and he had to retrieve it.

The phone call was what got him. That Texas Ranger Noonan really did a number on his mind. It was doing things to him. He'd breathe just once, quickly, and then he'd forget to breathe the next two or three times he should have in-between.

He thought of Annie and the kids.

God, how he missed them. All he wanted was to be back home with them, to have them all in his arms again.

He stood numbly in the shower, with the razor dangling from his hand. The noise of the water was loud and he was lost in it.

He got out of the shower, jerked a stiff white towel off the rack, rubbed a glow into his skin, and went over to the sink. In the mirror's merciless light he saw himself: hair streaming, eyes bloodshot, his bone-white, speckled egg of a face lined and empty.

He thought he heard something through the bathroom door again. It sounded like thuds and someone trying to hold back sobs.

Robert quickly threw on his jeans and shirt and went out into the room. It was hot and dark, and the reek of whiskey made the air sweetly sick.

His father was standing over Helen Garard's bed, and when he heard the bathroom door open he looked over his shoulder at Robert and smiled. It was the sort of smile Lazarus must have had after Jesus raised him from the dead.

Underneath his father, Helen Garard lay on the bed, her hands still bound to the bed post.

Her black skirt was pulled up past her hips and her fuzzy sweater was pushed up around her neck. Her pink panties were stretched down around her skinny thighs and one of her white knee socks was crumpled around her young ankle.

"What the fuck are you doing?" Robert shouted, throwing his father off the girl.

In the watery gold light of the room, the lines showed around Dick Haywood's eyes, but he held himself as straight as a tent pole.

"We were just getting to know each other a little better," he said with a saggy smile. His gaunt, angular face seemed stretched tighter over the bones. "Ain't that right, sugar?"

The girl's breasts were rising and falling in uneven breathing. Her mouth was twitching and her lower lip looked like it was going to melt on her chin.

Robert went over to her and untied her wrists. She brought them down quickly and straightened out her sweater and skirt and underthings.

"Are you okay?" Robert whispered to her.

She nodded, speechless, shaken with rough sobs.

Robert looked up hard at his father, dark glitter in his black eyes.

"What the fuck's the matter with you?"

Dick Haywood spread his hands and shrugged. "We were just gonna party a little. Ah, c'mon, don't tell me you weren't thinking about it? I seen the way you been looking at her."

Robert eyed his father slowly. "You're fucking crazy," he said with whispered vehemence. "You're a fucking crazy old man."

His father shrugged again. From the bedside table he drew the bottle of whiskey, offering it to Robert and the girl and shrugged again, unscrewing the cap.

"Jesus, my throat's sore as a bull's ass in fly time. Here's lead in the old pencil, huh?"

He tipped the bottle and took a long gulp.

"Ah-h, first of the day. That's always the best. 'Cepting for the last."

He smiled sourly and reached under his pillow and pulled out the .45.

"C'mon," he said. "We've got to hit the road if we want to make it home tonight. I don't want Annie all sore at me if I get you home late, son."

"What about me?" Helen Garard asked, her voice doing somersaults. "Are you going to let me go now?"

"Not just yet, sugar," Dick Haywood said, pointing the gun at her. "But I promise, we'll let you go pretty soon."

The girl looked up at Robert and he tried to tell her with his eyes that everything was going to be okay.

His father picked up the bottle again, took a long, last pull, finished it, and heaved it into the corner of the room. "There's another dead soldier."

He turned and opened the door and Robert and the girl followed him out of the room and into the parking lot. The glare of the morning sun hit them in the eyes like a clenched fist.

They hurried across the blacktop and by the time they reached the car they were all sweating. It was like a furnace outside, under that flood of blinding light falling from the sky, flashing from rows of windshields, from chrome handles and the smooth curves of enameled mudguards.

Robert's father opened the passenger door of the Volvo, pushed the girl in, and slid behind the wheel. He told Robert to get in the backseat. Then he put on a pair of old-fashioned white sunglasses—the kind Elvis Presley used to wear—and put the car in reverse, backed out and moved down the street toward Highway 60.

Chapter 33

The wind blowing through the open windows of the small car felt fine against the oppressive heat. Dick Haywood was hunched over the wheel madly and the girl, Helen Garard, sat on the front seat, her long brown hair flowing out of the open window like spilled root beer.

In the backseat, Robert lit a cigarette, guarding the match flame against the wind with cupped hands. His head was aching slightly and the first cigarette of the day had a bitter taste.

The car sliced the wind with the sound of simmering water. The highway passed under them like a black zebra with one white stripe.

Helen Garard kept looking back at Robert. She was scared. She knew the old man wasn't going to let her go. He was going to kill her the second they got near Amarillo.

Robert looked out the window at the passing landscape: oil fields; eerily dying or dead ghost towns; tattered billboards flashing in the sun. Hank Williams was on the radio singing:

Now Jonah got along in the belly of the whale,
Daniel in the lion's den.
But I know a man he didn't try to get along,

*And he won't get a chance again,
And that's all she wrote...*

He *had* to stop it.

He didn't have any other choice. He wouldn't be able to live with himself if he let anything happen to the girl.

He thought of his girls. Jenny and baby Grace. He thought of Annie. How he missed her. He never thought about it much, before when he was with her; you sort of take those things for granted until you have them no more. He thought of his son. Jack. He couldn't wait to get back home and throw the football around with him. Kid had a hell of an arm. Going to be a high school quarterback someday.

Robert looked at his watch. Eleven-thirty.

There was no traffic; except for an occasional car or semi-truck racing past them on the other side of the dusty highway.

They crossed the Tule River and sped through a little town called Happy, not much of a town, just a couple of churches, an old saloon, a filling station and a Hardee's restaurant.

Only seventy-five miles was between them until they reached the town of Wayside.

It'll all be over soon.

Could he really go through with it? Turning in his father?

He had to.

There was no other way.

Robert stared at the back of his father's gray head and at his bloodshot eyes in the rear view mirror.

Could he really trade his own dad in?

He thought about when he was a little kid and he'd play baseball with him, his father teaching him how to swing, how to throw, how to run the bases, all the things good fathers are supposed to do but don't always do; playing, teaching, laughing and loving. He remembered sitting around the television at night watching the Astros as his old man cussed at the screen and drank his bottles of Lone Star and smoked his Marlboro cigarettes. Those were the nights his mom and dad let him stay up past his bedtime and they were good times. Great times.

The little car raced toward its destiny. His father's destiny and his destiny. Helen Garard sat in the front seat, a frozen look of panic on her pretty, young, freckled face. It was her destiny too.

"When will you let me go?" she said, her voice so low it was almost unheard.

Dick Haywood looked over at her and smiled. "Oh, we're gonna let ya go, sugar. You just don't worry your pretty little self about that."

He held up his silver Zippo, snapped it open, and took out a battered pack of Marlboros.

"You want one, sugar?"

The girl swiped at a piece of hair that kept blowing in her face. She nodded her head.

Dick Haywood flipped up a cigarette and she reached over and took it. He smiled. He snapped the Zippo again, lit her cigarette first and then his.

"How long you been smoking?" he asked. "It's not good for you, you know? That's why they call 'em *cancer sticks.*"

Helen Garard inhaled eagerly on the cigarette, trying to sound braver than she was. "I started when I was twelve. I guess I wanted to be cool and just like the other girls in school. I wanted boys to think I was sexy. Now I can't quit the things."

Robert wondered if the girl was trying to be nice to his father so he'd let her go. But Robert knew he wouldn't let her go, not before he hurt her first. Hurt her real bad.

He hurt everybody sooner or later.

Robert looked out the window and the green fields and golden meadows were beautiful. He wished he could share this sight with someone, anyone—Annie, Jenny, Grace and Jack—anyone besides his father.

How he hated him. How he loved him.
He looked at his watch again. *11:57.*
Just about fifty miles now...

There was an old deserted motel up ahead on the right hand side of the road, barely distinguishable through the dust and sun. The windows were all closed up and the screen door hung askew on its hinges. On the side of the building there was an old pay phone, its dirty glass still reflecting in the sunshine.

"Pull over," Robert said.

"You got to pee?" his father asked.

"I'm gonna call home."

"What?"

"I'm calling Annie from that payphone over there."

His father winced. "Boy you really are pussy-whipped," he said, his gnarled gold teeth showing under his upper lip. "Can't you just call her on that little cell phone of yours?"

"You broke it last night," Robert said. "Remember, Dad?"

Dick Haywood ran a dirty hand over his skinny face. "Oh, yeah. I guess I did just that, didn't I?"

"Pull over," Robert told him.

"Okay, son. Don't get your britches in a bundle."

His father jerked the little car off the highway and onto the dusty road, swinging it in an arc in front of the closed-down motel.

Robert crawled out of the back seat. Helen Garard gave him a look, a look with her eyes that seemed to say: *Please, don't leave me here with him alone.*

Robert turned and slowly walked over to the booth, praying to God that the old payphone hadn't been ripped out and that it still worked.

Over his shoulder he heard his father call out: "Give Annie and the little ones my love, will ya, son?"

The thought almost made Robert's stomach tilt.

He crunched over the gravel driveway and drew the door of the phone booth open.

There it was; thank God, there it was!

The big black phone sat in its cradle like a baby waiting to get nursed. Robert picked it up and put it to his ear.

A dial tone. *There was a dial tone.* Maybe God was watching out for him after all.

He dialed zero and told the operator he'd like to make a person-to-person collect call. A female voice, completely devoid of femininity, told him: *one moment please.*

A second's silence, then the phone started ringing on the other end.

Robert held his breath and waited for Annie to pick up. He knew she had to be home. He had timed it, knowing she'd be there. He could see her face. Her big green eyes. The freckles on her nose. He could hear her voice even before she picked up.

Where is she? She's got to be home. Pick up. Goddamn it, Annie, pick up.

On the fourth ring, just before he was going to hang up, Annie's breathless voice came through the line.

"*Annie*—"

"Robert? Is that you? Where are you?"

"I'm close," he said, trying to keep his voice steady. "I'm on my way home, Annie—"

"Good. The kids will be thrilled to see you. They keep asking me when Daddy's coming home."

"Are they there now?" *She doesn't know. Thank, God. She doesn't know.*

"The girls are taking a nap," Annie said. "But Jack's here. Wanna talk to him?"

"Yeah. That'd be great."

He heard Annie take her mouth away from the phone and ask Jack if he wanted to talk. In the distance he heard his son ask who it was. Annie told him Daddy and he nearly screamed.

"Hello, Dad—?" he said into the phone.

"Yes, son, it's me," Robert said, trying to be strong, trying not to cry.

"When are you coming home, Dad? I miss you. We all miss you."

"I miss you too, son," Robert said breathlessly. "Are you being a good boy for your mom?"

"I think so, Daddy," Jack said proudly. "I helped her clean the basement this morning."

"You did?"

"Yep."

"That's great. How are your sisters?"

"Good. Jenny and me got into a fight. She took one of my dinosaurs without asking. But Mom says I got to share."

"She's right," Robert said with a smile. "Listen to your mom, she's always right."

"I know. When are you coming home, Daddy?"

"I'll be home soon, son."

"I love you, Dad."

"I love you, too, son."

"Bye, Dad."

"Bye, Jackie Boy. Can I talk to your mom again?"

He heard the boy drop the phone and call to his mom. "*Maahaam!*"

Annie picked up again and her voice never sounded more tender.

"I miss you, baby," Robert told her.

"I miss you, too," she said in a deeper voice. "You wouldn't believe how much I've missed you. I keep thinking about you all the time; you know what I mean?" She let out a little girl's giggle. "When you gonna be home, Robert?"

He looked over his shoulder at the car. His father was leaning his head out the window and smoking a cigarette. Helen Garard was sitting in the front seat, as far away as possible from him.

"I'll be home soon, baby," Robert said into the phone. "Real soon."

There was a long pause. Then slowly, Annie said:

"I love you, Robert Haywood. I love you so much."

"I love you, too, Annie. See you soon."

"See ya," she said, and hung up with a soft click.

Robert kept clutching the phone and staring out at the acres of green corn fields. He couldn't believe he was going to go through with this; couldn't believe it was done. *There was no turning back now.*

Some woman's voice was now speaking to him. A pre-recorded operator's voice instructing him politely to hang up the phone. It kept repeating itself, and then it moved unhesitatingly into a series of several sharp beeps.

Robert dropped the phone and let it swing.

The beeps continued as he slowly walked back to the car.

Chapter 34

It was almost high noon now. Lopez and Terry were parked out in an oil field behind the Sinclair filling station on Highway 60, just outside the small town of Wayside. The sun was out and it was a gorgeous day, except for the stink of cattle in the air.

"You think they'll show?" Lopez said, squinting down the highway through her expensive Ray Bans.

"They'll show," Terry said. "I could tell in Robert's voice. I could tell I had him."

"But it's his father," Lopez said. "His very own father. Think he'll go through with it?"

Terry took out a pack of cigarettes and handed one to her. He struck up a match and held it out to her in his shielded hands, then he shared the match and lit his own.

"Robert Haywood wants to go home," he said, puffing on his cigarette. "He wants to see his kids and fuck his wife, pardon my French, and he'll do anything to get there."

"Even if it means selling out his own father?" Lopez asked.

Terry nodded his head and squinted. "Yep. Wouldn't you? If you wanted to get back home to your wife and kids, and there was only one way to do it, wouldn't you do it? Wouldn't you sell him out?"

"I don't know," Lopez said in a low voice. "I guess it depends on the father."

"Bingo," Terry said, snapping his fingers. "And the last time I checked, Dick Haywood hasn't won any Father of the Year awards lately."

Lopez stared at him. "Would you do it?"

Terry stared back at her. "You mean turn in my father?" He laughed menacingly. "In a heartbeat. He wouldn't even have to commit murder. I'd turn the bastard in for spitting on the sidewalk."

Terry stared off into the glittering distance for a moment, his gaunt face sucking keenly on his cigarette.

"Robert Haywood is a smart boy," he said after a while. "He knows what he has to do. He'll show."

"I hope so," Lopez said. "Or Mister Jonathan Garard will have our ass. He wants his daughter back."

Terry turned his attention to the endless, empty road if front of them. Then he started humming softly:

"*She'll be coming 'round the mountain when she comes...*"

Chapter 35

Robert looked at his watch again. They had traveled another twenty minutes, another twenty miles. His father was reminiscing now, and Robert wished he would just shut the fuck up; it made it harder when the old man talked about the old times.

"You remember when me and you would play baseball, son? When you were little?" His father smiled and the three day's growth of beard on his haggard face made him look like a pirate. "Seems like just yesterday in some ways and like a million years in others. You had a helluva arm on ya, kid. I thought you'd grow up to pitch in the major leagues. And you could bat too. A helluva athlete you were; helluva athlete. And not just baseball; basketball, too. And football. I remember when you was in high school, me and your mama would go down to the football field every Friday night and watch you. You were your mama's pride and joy. She never missed a game."

Robert felt like a man being buried alive. He wanted to scream out: *stop it! Just stop it!* but he knew no one would hear him anyway.

They were getting closer now and his father kept rambling on about the good old days which Robert remembered were pretty good, but pretty shitty too.

He looked out the side window at the long ranges of clouds, thick as beaten egg-whites, moving in the afternoon sky. Through the cracks of clouds, the dome of sky was as clear as bluing water.

The highway still stretched emptily.

On the left was a signpost: *Wayside...13 miles.*

Thirteen more miles, Robert thought. Old unlucky thirteen.

A car shot up over the rise ahead, hurtled toward them. The sun reflected off the approaching hood and it sparkled like a diamond.

The car passed with a swooshing sound.

I got time to turn back, Robert told himself. *Just bail out on the whole thing. Tell Dad to get off the highway and turn around.*

But then what? What do I do then?

Helen Garard looked at him over the front seat. God was she pretty, her long dark hair flowing out like that, and her petite little angel face, so kissable and so scared. Her small even features had the jewel-like splendor that tiredness and fright gives to the very young.

What would I be going through if it was my daughter that was taken?

Robert couldn't look at Helen's face anymore. He looked past her shoulder at some vague spot in the distance.

He brought his eyes back from the distance, looked at Helen Garard gravely for a brief moment, looked away again.

And then there it was, out there in the middle of nowhere, as strange and out of place as snow in summer or rain at harvest time.

A lonely sign on the side of the highway:

Welcome to Wayside.

They passed the bright green road sign and stayed on the highway that ran parallel to the tiny Main Street, if you could call it that.

Robert didn't see an old-time filling station with a barbeque joint on the other side. He wondered if that smug Texas Ranger knew what the hell he was talking about. Maybe the bastard had made a mistake. In some ways Robert hoped that he had, and in other ways he hoped that he hadn't. He wanted to end this thing; right here, right now.

They swung around the tiny town and his father got the car moving up to a steady sixty again.

The wind was still blowing through the open windows and Helen Garard looked like she might fall asleep again.

Then they hit a rise in the highway and when they reached the top and started to descend, Robert saw it, gleaming in the sun just above the horizon.

The old-time filling station.

He stared at it as they drew closer, and he thought it looked like that painting, *Gas,* by Edward Hopper.

With its long shadows, dark road, big green pines hovering above it, the place conveyed the loneliness of travel and an atmosphere of an almost eerie solitude. The big green dinosaur soaring above the blue letters on the Sinclair sign was raked with sunlight and teaming with tension. It was like a theatrical scene before the curtain rises—the drama waiting to unfold...

"Do you need to fill the car up with gas?" Robert asked from the backseat.

His father stared through the dusty windshield, then down at the gas gauge.

He burped softly once, and then said, "Yeah, I suppose we could top her off."

He switched on the blinker and pulled the car slowly off the highway and onto the gravel driveway of the filling station. Across the highway was the old restaurant, just like Noonan had said: nothing but a roadside barbeque joint, like a million others you see on any other Texas highway. Beyond that was farm land, sage grass and brownweed; far-reaching woods of green and burnt orange.

Under the filling station's red-colored pumps, swirling insects clouded the naked bulbs in the sun. Crickets in the roadside grass sounded like the buzz of electrical wires. There was a car under the shed of the filling station on the right. A man in coveralls stood beside the red pumps twisting the handles. He was tall and lean, with a trimmed body and ice blue eyes. He looked too clean and too white and too strong to be working at a gas station in the middle of nowhere. He was wearing a sleeveless shirt with the name *Willie* stenciled above his heart. Yeah right, like this guy's real name was *Willie,* Robert thought.

Willie walked around to the side of the car, and asked, "Waddle it be?"

"Fill 'er up," Dick Haywood said.

The man smiled a little smile but his eyes were dark and turned inward, thinking. He looked inside the car and in his face Robert could see the reflection of the brain working behind it.

"Sure thing, buddy," Willie said vaguely. He pointed across the highway to the old barbeque joint. "If yer hungry, that place over yonder serves a mean roast beef on rye."

"Thanks much," Dick Haywood said. "But we're kinda in a hurry, pal."

The man was lifting the pump now and sticking it in the side of the car. "You can get it to go," he said, his eyes moving back and forth between them. "Best barbeque south of Kansas City."

The pump was ticking away.

Robert moved in his seat.

"You hungry?" he asked his father. "I could run over there and grab us a couple of those barbeque sandwiches."

His father took out a cigarette and lit it.

"Nah, I ain't all that hungry."

"I'm starving," the girl said.

Thank God, Robert screamed silently to himself. Thank God she said something. He could have kissed her right there.

He had to get the girl away from here, into the restaurant. That's what Noonan had told him to do.

"You want to go across the street with me?" Robert asked the girl.

His father squinted on his cigarette and perked up his head.

"We could get a couple of sandwiches and take a potty break," Robert said.

The girl shrugged her shoulders. "Yeah, I guess so. I got to pee real bad."

"Hold on a second," Dick Haywood said, throwing his cigarette out the open window. "You two ain't going nowhere."

"C'mon, Dad," Robert said, forcing a chuckle out of himself. "What are we going to do, run off to Mexico and elope? Where are we going to go? We're out here in the middle of nowhere."

Robert watched to see if any of this was having an effect on his father.

Then he said, "You trust me, don't ya, Dad? I haven't done anything to make you not trust me...*have I?*"

His father thought it over for a moment, then a little smile touched his skinny lips. It was like he had just remembered something, something pleasant from a long time ago.

"All right," he said, reaching over the seat and rubbing Robert's hair. "Grab me one of those famous roast beef's while you're in there."

"Sure thing, pop," Robert said, getting out of the car.

Helen Garard opened her door and slowly got out. She reached for the sky with her small arms and stretched her stiff legs. Dick Haywood looked over at her skinny smooth belly sticking out of her sweater and at that fabulous ass. Too bad he couldn't get any of that. He would've rather had a piece of *that* to eat than the barbeque sandwich.

Helen walked in front of the car and stood next to Robert.

Dick Haywood stuck his head out the window of the car. "Say, son, before you go, I want to tell you something."

Robert walked around the car and leaned his head inside the window and he could smell the stale smoke on his father's breath.

"Yeah, Dad, what is it?"

His father tilted his head and smiled crookedly. "You know that money I was talking about? That loot I got buried in an abandoned shack outside the Nemadji State Forest? I meant what I said, son, about splitting it with you when we get back home. Splitting it right down the middle. You and Annie won't have to worry about money for a long time."

Robert padded his father on the arm.

"Sure, Dad." His voice was hoarse; he couldn't get it much above a whisper. He stopped for a deep breath, then went on in a different tone, "*I love you, Dad.*"

The words just slipped out, like water through a crumbling dam.

His father looked up at him and stared into his eyes. "You haven't said that to me in over twenty years." He paused, and there was this contented smile on his face. He looked so happy, happier than Robert had ever seen him before in his whole life.

"I love you, too, son," he said, and Robert thought he might start to cry.

Before he could, he turned away from the car and grabbed Helen Garard gently by the elbow.

They started walking and their feet crunched on the gravel parking lot.

Robert looked back once before they crossed the highway to the restaurant and he saw his father sitting by himself inside the car, smoking contently on a fresh cigarette.

For a moment Robert had a brief memory of his father sitting in the sunshine on the back porch of their house on Cherry Avenue, smoking a cigarette and blowing smoke rings up to the gods.

A semi horn blasted Robert back into the present. It passed them closely on the highway. It was the only vehicle they saw on this lonely stretch of land.

He took the girl and they crossed the blacktop and walked more quickly to the doors of the restaurant.

He looked back again, and now he could see a car approaching the filling station from up on the hill. It was one of those beige plain Jane cars. A government car. *An FBI car.*

When his father saw the approaching car he sat up stiffly in his seat, and looked back once at Robert. He couldn't be sure, but Robert thought he saw a little knowing smirk on the old man's lips.

Did he know? Could he know?

Robert grabbed the girl and pushed her inside the doors of the restaurant.

"Hey—" she cried out, but stopped when she saw the look in Robert's eyes.

She followed his gaze and stood silently next to him, watching as the beige car sped toward the filling station pumps.

Robert saw his father reach under the seat for the gun and he held out his palm against the glass of the restaurant's door, as if that would stop what was about to happen...

Chapter 36

Dick Haywood got out of the car just as the beige Ford came to a screeching stop, sending up a plume of dust all around him.

The filling station attendant, whose real name was not *Willie,* but Special Agent Peter Huddleston, a six-year veteran of the FBI and a decorated ex-Marine who had served his time in Desert Storm, came out from behind the gas pumps and was going for his gun.

But Dick Haywood had a line on him.

He raised the old Colt and shot Huddleston in the eye.

Huddleston just stood there for a moment, as the red spot in his eye started spreading across his face like a spiderweb.

Then he fell to his knees and toppled over onto the ground.

The people in the restaurant, including Robert and the girl, heard the shot, thunderous and somehow divorced from time. There was that instant when nobody makes a sound, when it almost seems as if there will never again be any sound—after the sound of a gun.

It was all going down so fast, but at the same time, it was like it was happening in slow-motion.

Terry Noonan was out of the Ford now, his right hand reaching inside his coat pocket for the .50 gauge AE autoloader, his *Grace of God.*

Dick Haywood turned and brought the Colt up quickly and shot him in the belly.

A red mass exploded like a sunburst.

A surprised look came across Terry's face, as though he couldn't believe he had just been shot.

He dropped his gun into the dirt and grabbed his bleeding gut with both hands. He looked down at the gaping hole, then he fell on his butt and sloped against the side of the car.

All he could see was the haze of air. The sky was falling on top of him and he couldn't push it away. Just another trip, sliding out through the cracks. The bullet had split him wide open and his soul was furling its way out.

Lopez was leaning across the hood of the Ford, her big SIG Sauer .380 pointed directly at Dick Haywood's head.

"Throw down your weapon!" she shouted. "Throw it down now!"

A smile touched Dick Haywood's thin, wrinkled, tan face. He stood there, amid the blood and dust, and smiled his contented smile.

"Throw it down, Haywood," Lopez screamed again.

But he just stood there, like he didn't hear her.

Then he turned his head slowly and looked across the highway into the glass windows of the little restaurant.

Dick Haywood's cold gray eyes locked with his son's and he let out another little gold-toothed smile.

Then he lowered his head gently and turned his gaze back to Lopez. She had the big gun on him, but he could see that her hands were shaking.

He held out his arms and shrugged his shoulders. His long face was serious, but not hard. He said to her:

"I've already come this far, sugar..."

"No...!" Lopez shouted.

Dick Haywood's hand was moving slowly toward her...

He whispered: "This had to end sooner or later; it may as well end now..."

Dick Haywood raised the Colt in his hand and started aiming it at her.

Lopez squinted in the sun and squeezed the trigger four times.

The first shot hit Dick Haywood in the left shoulder and he let out a sound like "*Uuumph*" as his arm flung itself behind him and he stumbled.

The second shot took him in the thigh and he stopped for a brief second, but then he got his legs moving again and he kept coming.

The third shot sliced through the side of his cheek but didn't seem to have any effect on him.

The fourth and final shot hit him in the neck with a sickening sound and the bullet went out through the other side in a spew of blood.

Dick Haywood stopped then and dropped the Colt into the dust.

His eyes were red and watery. His legs wobbled and pain filled his head.

Light flared—blinding white light that filled the world.

Then it was dark.

Chapter 37

He woke to blinding light.

Terry cracked his eyes open a little further. The first thing he saw was the light and the movement.

Where the hell am I? Am I dead?

Then he saw the girl in the white dress and white stockings sitting in the corner of the room. She was reading a paperback by Arthur Mayse and when Terry made a little noise she put the book down and stood up. Her legs were fantastic and the rest of her wasn't bad either. She had long curly blonde hair and her big full lips were painted in a light shade of pink.

He thought: Well, if I *am* dead, then I've gone to heaven.

The girl smiled with those big red lips and walked over to his bed. She put her hand on his arm.

"*Am I in Heaven?*" he said through dry, cracked lips.

He felt like a branding iron had been stuck up his ass and was bursting inside his guts.

"No," the girl said in a sweet, syrupy voice. "You're in Dallas General."

"The hospital?" Terry asked.

The girl smiled and nodded her head. She took his blood pressure and his vitals and he couldn't help looking down her blouse as she bent over him.

"You were shot in the stomach," she said. "Do you remember anything at all?"

Terry nodded his head.

The girl went on: "They flew you down here from Wayside in a helicopter."

"Fucking helicopters," Terry whispered to himself.

"What's that?"

"Nothing, honey."

"You're going to be just fine," the pretty nurse said. "Thing's didn't look too good at first but you were a fighter. It took them three hours of surgery to pull that bullet out of your tummy." She smiled again and pulled the comfortable hospital blanket up to his chin. "There you go, all tucked in."

"What about my partner?" Terry asked, concerned that Lopez was hurt in the gunfight.

"She's outside," the girl said. "Want me to bring her in?"

Relief flooded through him like a hit of H, but it was better than he'd ever felt before. He really did care about Lopez. He almost couldn't fucking believe it. She had gotten into his head.

He nodded to the nurse and she walked out of the room. A few seconds later the door opened again and Lopez walked in slowly.

She was wearing a two-tone Tahari business suit and her dark hair was pulled back off her face. Terry usually didn't subscribe to clichés, but when he saw her he thought of the one about being a sight for sore eyes.

She was carrying a little stuffed Scooby-Doo in her hands.

"Who's your friend?" Terry asked.

Lopez looked down at Scooby and smiled.

"It's for you," she said, holding it out in front of her. "It's all I could find in the store downstairs."

She walked over to the bed and put Scooby down by Terry's feet.

"You okay?" he asked.

She seemed to let out a little sob, then she nodded her head.

"I thought you were going to die," she said and her brown eyes shone.

He raised his head a little off the pillow and smiled up at her. "Hey, I'm too stubborn to die."

Another goddamn cliché.

Lopez smiled back at him and swiped a tear that was on her cheek.

"What happened to Haywood?" Terry asked.

Lopez turned her head and looked out the window. The sun was shining brilliantly and it looked like another God-awful hot Texas day.

Terry said without emotion: "Is he dead?"

Lopez nodded her head, but didn't say anything, didn't look at him. He knew what she was going through after her first kill. He went through the same thing just two years ago.

"It gets better," he said. "The guilt goes away. Trust me on that one."

She tried to smile again, but it came out all crooked.

Terry moved his feet a little over on the bed. "Sit down."

Lopez lowered herself to the edge of the bed and crossed her legs.

"Helen Garard made it home okay?" Terry asked.

"Yeah, she's safe at home."

"That's good," he said. "And Robert Haywood? Whatever happened to him?"

"He's going home," Lopez said. "The FBI kept its promise. He got immunity for helping us. The Bureau slapped him on the wrist and sent him home."

"He lost his father," Terry said, in a low voice.

"But he got to keep his wife and kids," Lopez said with a note of finality. She didn't want to talk about it anymore.

Terry was thoughtful for a moment, his head still spinning from the morphine drip in his arm. Everything was falling into place and still he couldn't really grasp it.

He was tired and his whole body ached, yet, he couldn't stop thinking about Lopez and if he'd ever get to see her again now that the case was finished.

He yawned cavernously.

"I should go," Lopez said. "You look tired."

She moved to get up but he reached out and said: "Don't go."

She sat back down on the hospital bed and the shuffling of her two-tone suit sounded like a gentle rain.

"I know I acted badly at that bar the other night—" Terry said.

She smiled and rubbed his arm playfully. "What the hell are you talking about? You act badly all the time, Noonan!"

"I just—" He let out a big sigh. "I just want you to know that I really respect you. I know I didn't show it that night. I never meant to hurt you. I just can't stop thinking about you."

She blushed. "Boy, you really must be spinning from that morphine. You're starting to sound like one of those gushy Country and Western songs that you love so much."

"Don't go," he said, and reached out for her again.

"I'm not."

"My ears are ringing," he said.

She bent toward him and touched his face. He reached out for her and brought her toward him.

The perfect, narrow streets of Amarillo looked different somehow. He couldn't put his finger on it, but they had changed. No, that wasn't exactly right. He was the one who had changed, and his surroundings had merely changed with him.

He sat in the backseat of the taxi and watched as the perfect lawns and the red brick homes slid past, and his stomach began to get jumpy.

He couldn't wait to see the kids. He could picture them now, laughing and jumping up and down when they saw him.

And Annie.

Her beautiful smile and those shining green eyes peeking out from under the wisps of blonde hair.

He wondered what she would say or do when she saw him, wondered if there would be any apprehension toward him.

Robert sat back in the taxi and watched as the addresses began their slow countdown to his house.

The sun was hanging in the west, just above the treetops, and the air was heavy and hot and tainted with the evocative sounds of children playing in the street.

The taxi turned off the main intersection and as it rattled down the familiar streets, Robert could almost feel his house getting closer, like a magnet.

He saw the old familiar landmarks—the park where he threw the football around with Jackie, the magnolia tree that little Jenny loved to climb, the corner butcher shop where they walked to as a family on Sunday mornings to buy T-bones and the Sunday paper.

The taxi turned again and then he could see his house, down the block on the right.

A low moan got caught in the back of Robert's throat and for a minute he thought he might actually break out and cry. But he didn't.

The taxi pulled up to the side of the street in front of his driveway and he got out and paid the guy. Then he turned around and started slowly walking up his driveway.

He was about halfway there when the front door burst open and Jack and Jenny came sprinting out after him. He couldn't hold back the tears now as he bent down and clutched them both in his arms. He buried his face in their sweet smelling hair and kissed them all over.

He looked up and saw Annie standing in the doorway holding baby Grace.

He smiled and Annie smiled back. He went over to her and kissed the top of Grace's head.

"Hello, stranger," Annie said, and there was a strained eager quality in her voice and in her eyes when she looked at him.

"I missed you," he said.

"I'm glad you're home," she said. "I missed you, too."

He caught her to him then with unexpected fierceness, and they clung together for a brief moment that seemed like an eternity.

Robert kissed her hungrily, twice on the mouth and once above the eye.

"I love you," he said. "I'm sorry I brought this on you, Annie."

She didn't say anything, but she kissed him back, and that was all the forgiveness he needed for now.

Epilogue

Out in the backyard the smell of T-bone steaks, sizzling on the grill with the fat dripping down on the coals, wafted through the blue air.

The kids were playing—running and rolling down the long grassy hill in the backyard and laughing.

Robert stood staring into the Coleman with a long fork in one hand and a bottle of beer in the other. Around his waist was a long white apron with the words "GRILL MASTER GENERAL" printed in red letters across the front.

He smiled as he watched the kids playing.

Annie came out of the sliding glass doors and walked across the patio holding baby Grace in one hand and two fresh bottles of Corona—one for Robert and one for herself—in the other.

Robert smiled as she handed him his beer. Then they both stood silently staring at the steaks on the grill.

"Looks good," Annie said, smiling and sipping at her beer.

"Yeah."

She looked over her shoulder at the kids now hanging off the Jungle Jim. She bent down and set Grace on the patio with a few chew toys to keep her busy.

"Any prospects today?" she asked Robert, squinting into the fading sun.

It had been four months since it all happened. They buried his father and then tried to go on living as if nothing ever happened. But then one day Longwell—*Mr. Moneybags*—called Robert into his office. Robert knew it wasn't going to be good.

And it wasn't.

Longwell told him it was nothing personal, but they were going to have to let him go.

Yeah right, nothing personal, Robert had thought. They said it was because of their sloping budget, but he knew it was because of all the negative publicity surrounding the bank after what had happened to him out in the desert. They gave him his two weeks' notice and then shoved him out the door with only half of his accumulated pension.

He had been hitting the want ads pretty hard for the last two months, but still no job had materialized.

"I have an interview on Monday," he said, smiling at Annie.

"That's great, Robert. Who's it with?"

"Wells Fargo."

They were silent for a moment. Then Annie reached out and touched his arm.

"I hope this one pans out, Robert," she said slowly, thickly, hopelessly. "I'm scared. Our mortgage is already three months into foreclosure and the bill collectors are practically banging down the front door."

"I know, Annie."

He felt bad for her. He was sure this wasn't what she had in mind when he had promised her the world.

He looked at her slowly, with an empty up-from-under look. "It'll all work out, Annie. Let's try not to think about it tonight. Let's just enjoy these steaks, have a few more beers and just relax. Maybe put the kids to bed early, if you know what I mean?"

She smiled and blushed and leaned over to kiss him.

"I love you, Robert Haywood," she said in a voice that shook a little.

The house was silent. It was after midnight and the kids had been sleeping soundly for several hours. After five or six beers and a heavy round of lovemaking, Annie was passed out on the bed. The covers were thrown back, her white cotton nightgown wedged above her thighs and the almond scent of her body wrapped itself around Robert's neck like a noose. She was so beautiful, like that sleeping girl in the book *A Little Princess.*

But Robert couldn't sleep. He kept thinking about that shack his father told him about out in the Nemadji State Forest.

The one with all the money hidden it.

He stared at the ceiling and lay awake for hours, hearing the sounds of a barking dog in the neighbor's backyard.

He turned over in bed and closed his eyes, but the thought of the shack and the money in it kept breaking into his mind by the tiny unlocked door of sleep.

A quarter of a million dollars. At least.

He could pay off the foreclosure with that kind of cash, get caught up on the credit cards, put a little away for the children's college funds, and still have plenty left over.

Finally, Robert threw off the covers and silently got dressed, looking back once at Annie, but she was still sleeping soundly, snoring softly in her sweet way.

He snuck out of the room and down the stairs like Ali Baba in the night. He took a gym bag out of the front hall closet and put on his old boots he used for working in the yard.

At the front door, he put his hand on the knob, hesitated, and then went out into the moonlight.

He got into his pickup, lifted the key to the ignition, but his hand was shaking.

Drive, said the voice inside his head.

He drove for over an hour in the dark night, chugging coffee out of a silver Thermos in the hope of pacifying his stomach and his soul, nothing to keep him company but the sound of the tires on the road and the radio turned down low.

A narrow rocky road dropped down from the highway and ran along the flank of the hill above Hanging Horn Lake. The tops of cabins showed here and there in the midst of tall pines.

Robert pulled his car off the highway and took the road north into the Nemadji forest.

The lake was deep blue and silent, except for the chugging of an outboard motor somewhere in the far-off distance.

The trees grew deeper and deeper and the road narrowed to almost one lane. It was so dark out here that Robert had to switch on his high beams. He drove slowly, inspecting the woods on both sides of the road.

Everything was still, except for the breeze overhead in the treetops.

He continued driving until the road came to a dead end. Then, taking a flashlight from the glove compartment and the gym bag from the backseat, he got out of the car and walked into the woods.

Once in the heavy growth, he turned on the flashlight and soon found the path his father had told him to take to the abandoned shack.

As he proceeded deeper into the darkness he felt the fear and restlessness he always experienced when he was alone in the woods. When he was a little kid his father used to take him hunting and leave him alone in a stand deep within the Nemadji woods. Robert always hated it, and he hated it now.

He paused for a moment, surrounded by the profound silence of the forest. Then, pushing ahead, he saw another small trail branching to the right.

He moved down the path, now focused totally on what awaited him at the end of the rainbow.

There were stars of spangled sapphire, and there were lilies, and violets wet with dew. Someone had laid duckboards across the marshy area of the path so that it was passable.

Would it still be there after all these years? Had it been discovered by a hunter or a camper or some kids partying in the woods?

He came to a clearing, and at the edge he stopped and turned off the flashlight.

The abandoned shack stood under a tall pine, just like his father had said it would.

The front door was missing and the windows had long disappeared. There was tall grass and weeds in the front and a dull patch of something that had once been a lawn at the back. There was a wire clothes line and wooden steps leading up to the gaping front door.

The moonlight showed all this.

Robert waited under the tall pine for a moment, watching and listening. It was stagnantly quiet, except for the rustling in the trees far overhead. His whole body was shivering with nerves.

He stepped into the clearing and quietly approached the shack. Then he went up the wooden steps, crossed the rickety porch as quietly as he could, stood at the threshold for a moment, and then went in...

The puffy pink clouds on the horizon shone like smoke in the purple and blue sky. The sun would be making its appearance soon.

As he drove home Robert felt alive for the very first time in months, maybe years.

He parked his truck in the garage, killed the engine, got out and took the gym bag out of the backseat. He left his dirty work boots out in the garage and went into the house.

Everybody was still asleep and that was good.

He went upstairs and peeked in the kids' rooms. They were still sleeping like characters in a fairy tale.

Then he went down the hall to his bedroom and stood at the door for a moment, staring at Annie still sleeping on the big bed, snoring softly.

He put the gym bag in the closet, took off his clothes, pulled back the covers, and crawled in bed next to his wife.

The End

Jason Holscher was almost born in the backseat of a 1967 Plymouth Belvedere station wagon on the outskirts of San Angelo, Texas. He now resides in Cannon Falls, Minnesota. Dead Man's Blues is his third novel.

Made in the USA
Lexington, KY
12 June 2012